Dope Girl

The beginning

Sa'id Salaam

Dope Girl

ISBN-10:
1484874129

Cover Design: Dynasty cover me

Join me on facebook - saidsalaam fan page

Twitter @ salaamsaid

Dedicated to Zakiyyah Salaam

Acknowledgements

First all praise is for Allah Lord of everything.
Mommy Deidra, Grandma Rainey, Daughter Jessica, Sons Erv-
G, and Ramel J aka Doobie daddy, The grands Gavin and Aliya.
Sister Satira, Brothers William, Carl, Mark, Akia. Cousins,
Aunts, Uncles, Nieces and Nephews.

My fellow authors especially but not limited to: Amira
Queenpen, Treasure Blue, K'wan, Ashley and Jacquavious,
Young Lit, Leo Sullivan, Author Quianna (Salaams Sister), Ms.
Shan, Hood Chronicles, Nika Michelle, Marie Norfleet, Kelvin
Jackson, Fire and Ice, Sabrina Eubanks, Katavious Ellis,
Rasheed, Chrishawn Simpson, Author LaRedeaux, Tremaine
Johnson, Julia Press Simsons, Mike-O, Patron Gold, Tina
Nance, Jerrice Owens, Arabia Dover, Joe Awsum, Felisha
Bradshaw, niecy coulture, Paige Green, Cole Hart, David
Weaver, Angela Day, Eyone Willians, Taquila Thompson, The
ladies of OOSA, DC bookdiva, Cash Money Content, and
errbody else.

Renee Lamb, Chuncky, Farryn Grant, Stephanie Tarrer, Judith
Sims, Aniya Brown, Sharon Lady Shay, Nicole Santa Cruz, Detra
Young, Zaneta Powell, Sandy "The Book- Connoisseur" Barrett
Sims, Swiperda Foxest, Denise (Aunt DG) Gilliam, Gabrielle
Dotson, Dee Boggess, Katrice Mathis, Kitty Galore, Roslyn
Reed, Tee-Tee Samuels, Dawn Mellette, Christina, Roneesha

Wynn, Shemika Jones Lee O'neil, Kenisha Parker, Erica Black butterfly Hale, Darke N Lovely, Stephanie Thompson, Michelle Rawls, Adrienne Jones, Papaya, La La, Christina Willians, Tampeka Lester, Marcia Benson, and everyone I'm forgetting right now.

My Editor the lovely Sandy "The Book- Connoisseur" Barrett Sims, Thanks for your time energy and attention to detail.

Andrew (Mezan) Mayes, Nichole Kagee, both Abdul Qawi (s), Abdullah Hakim, Amin,My dude Yi you came through in the ninth inning and helped more than you know!, Jihad, Haleem, Rafi, Adul Nur, B-5, Dro, Bop, Ali, Rasheed, Abdur-Rasheed (J.u.), 1440, Basir, Nasir, Amir, Amira, Adla Berry, Abu Na'eem, April Na'eema, Aminah, Yara Umm Shahadah,.

Peace.…
In the name of God, most gracious, most merciful
By the token of time.

Verily mankind is in loss.

Except for those who believe and do righteous deeds, and recommend each other to truth, and recommend each other to patience.

Chapter 1

Kathy Johnson was a whore long before she had ever gotten paid for sex. As a young girl she sought out laps that paid to be sat in. She did quite well as a child and always had money for candy and treats.

When puberty hit, she filled out in all the right places and she was in high demand. She would gladly give it up to the boys just because she liked sex and loved attention. She was in such high demand, that one boy had only offered a few dollars to skip the long line leading to her vagina. That offer opened up a whole new world.

Boys paid what they could, but once the men of the small town got wind of the fine young thing who fucked for free, they wanted in as well, literally.

Kathy was Jet black and built for speed. She was too poor for perms, but the head full of thick course hair only added to her appeal.

Not to mention, the high temperatures in the Mississippi Delta called for as little clothing as possible. The tiny shorts showcasing a lovely mound of black ass cleavage could not be ignored.

Soon, she was fucking every day, except for her monthly cycle. That was known locally as "Head Week". The fee for admission varied from a few dollars here or a ride over there. Whatever was needed could be easily obtained with a spread of her big pretty thighs. Practice makes perfect, and her head was soon the stuff legends were made of. She had what's referred to down south as 'fiyah head'.

A local dope boy called Skee-bo happened across some of that good head and put her on his payroll. She would sit around the trap house with him listening to the rapper D-Lite or watching Animal on DVD, and giving dynamite blow jobs on call. She was like 'on demand'; men would die for a blow job button on the remote. Industry would come to a grinding halt if such a thing were ever invented.

Skee-bo decided to save a little cash, and instead, paid her in crack. It took a little talking into and training, but once she'd gotten that first blast the game had changed.

Fucking for favors was gone with the wind. It now required hard cash to pay for hard rock to handle your hard cock. She would stay in the trap houses for weeks on end sexing and smoking.

Her sweet-sixteenth birthday was spent with her being passed around a crack house. It would have been sad, but she was so far out of touch she didn't know what month it was.

Kathy wasn't the only teen crack whore in town. Her friend Jahilya followed her into the cesspool she called "life", and was soon in the trenches of drug addiction and prostitution. They were the Cagney and Lacy of crack whores.

Pussy is, and always has been a commodity, and as such falls prey to the laws of supply and demand. When the demand for sex was low and the dick supply dwindled, the girls turned to stealing.

The ebb and flow of customers was directly influenced by the paydays of the local industries. The plants paid on the 1st and the 15th and business boomed. Other times of the month, not so much.

"Ooh I know!" Jahilya announced triumphantly as she did when inspiration struck. The girl was dumb, so an idea, any idea, was news. "We can go down to the department store and steal!"

Stealing from the small towns, even smaller department stores was a silly act of desperation. For one, they didn't carry much of anything of value, then, everyone knew everyone, their mothers, fathers, grandmothers, etc, etc…

"Ok!" Kathy eagerly agreed, and off they went.

"Hey Kay, how's your mama?" The overweight and under worked security guard inquired cheerfully upon seeing the girls enter. She, like everyone else in town, was extremely fond of her father Deacon Johnson and mother Sister Clara.

"Fine ma'am," Kathy guessed. She hadn't been home and had no clue on how they were doing.

In this small town everyone knew everyone else's business which made the guard wonder what Kathy was doing in the store; she certainly wasn't shopping.

Her suspicions proved true as she discreetly followed the wayward girls through the aisles. The amateur thieves stole things they liked instead of stuff that could be traded for the cash that could be traded for dope that would trade their sobriety for inebriation.

She could only shake her head as she watched them conceal trinkets under their skimpy clothing. The guard summoned the police who responded quickly in the relatively crime free town.

"This is easy!" Jahilya cheered as they waddled, laden with goods towards the front door.

"I know right! Let's drop this stuff off and come back for more!" Kathy agreed.

"Hey mista Mann," they sang sweetly as they saw the local beat cop posted outside. He had tricked with both girls before and hated what was coming next.

"Y'all gals stealing?" He asked, looking at the bulge in their clothing.

"No," the girls sang again in unison.

"Well, Ms. Judy seems to thank different, y'all go back inside."

They were taken to a back office and relieved of the stolen merchandise. Officer Mann was rock hard at the thought of sexing them both for letting them off with a firm warning. If Ms. Judy hadn't alerted the manager he would have spent the rest of his shift with the two girls.

The manager Mrs. Tombs knew the two tramps were the reason her husband brought home less than his take- home pay. Not to mention, he didn't have any use for her after tricking with them.

"I want these girls arrested!" she demanded, deflating the cop's penis. "I will personally come by and sign a statement. A message must be sent!"

The county judge had pity on the petty thieves. He knew they both came from broken homes and couldn't pay bail or fines. Not broken homes as in divorced, but broke as in nobody had much money, especially not money to waste on this foolishness.

"I sentence you girls to a year probation, stay out of trouble, and you can stay out of the jail!" He boomed down on the girls.

It was of course an exercise of futility. The notion of putting a drug addict on probation was built upon the same platform of the boomerang. No matter how hard or far you threw it, it was coming right back.

Knowing that the terms of the probation meant being drug free, the girls were immediately fugitives. Longs Mississippi didn't have many fugitives so they were high on the list.

No one searched for the girls harder than Officer Mann. He had no plans on cuffing them when he caught up with them; he wanted to fuck them both. That's exactly what he did when fate finally intertwined their paths.

"Hey gals!" Don't y'all run, ya hear!" The cop said as he lucked up on both of them.

They had just left the local trap house with several sucked dicks worth of crack in their pockets. Instinct told them to run, but the look in the deputies eyes told them his motive.

"Yes sir," they said together, as if trained.

"Y'all gals know y'all in trouble. The Judge issued warrants for the both of you," he said sounding all official, even though his dick was so hard it hurt. "Hop on in and let's see can we work something out."

"Okay," they sang and hopped in the police car.

The 'something' the cop wanted to work out was their firm young bodies. He took them over to a secluded field and took turns fucking them between rows of turnip and mustard greens.

Deputy Mann worked overtime that night. The citizens of Longs Mississippi were on their own that night. The deed grew tedious for the girls with dope on hand demanding to be smoked. Finally, the cop burst one last nut and was satisfied.

"Ok, I'ma let you gals go, but y'all steer clear of town and 'specially the sto'," he said sternly. "I'll meet y'all right back here on Saturday."

"Not for free you won't," Kathy said under her breath, as she waved goodbye. They decided they would smoke a few rocks right there before heading back to town.

"We go now?" The lead migrant worker asked with an eager smile and fist full of dollars. He and several others heard the sounds of sex from their cabins and had gone out to investigate.

When they saw the cop giving the girls the business, they wanted to give them some business too. They rushed back to the cabin and collected what didn't get wired to El Salvador.

"Eww no!" Jahilya frowned at the thought of having sex with the field hands. She was young enough to still be in the 'cute boy' stage and ignored the money in their hands.

Kathy followed her friend and turned the men down. They smoked their little rocks, and went back in search of more cocks. The girls walked back to town.

Jahilya's luck took a turn for the worst, and she was caught by the towns black cop deputy, Thom; Uncle Thom, as he was known because he hated black folks. He couldn't even stand looking in the mirror because of that black bastard staring back at him.

"Guess I'll suck yo' thang for you," Jahilya said in surrender. That gave her another charge of solicitation.

"I warned ya," The Judge said sympathetically. Since she was back in the system he had no choice but to revoke her probation.

She was actually blessed for the year in prison the Judge sentenced her to. It was a reprieve of sorts and served to save her from herself. It was just enough time to break the addiction that would have ultimately, otherwise killed her.

Kathy on the other hand wasn't so lucky. She remained free to destroy herself. When the small police force made it their business to clear their only outstanding warrant, they turned up the heat.

"Don't brang yo' ass round here no more," the dope boy warned when she stopped to cop. "Them folks been by here err' day looking for you."

He took her money but made it clear that she wasn't welcome. It was enough that the cops turned a blind eye to his dealing, but he would not harbor a fugitive. He, like the bootlegger and whore house, was tolerated. In America everyone has a vice, so why be a hypocrite?

Deputy Mann liked young black girls, while Uncle Thom liked kissing white people's pink asses. The judge liked little boys, and the Sheriff wore panties under his uniform;only in America.

Kathy wandered aimlessly until she remembered the men in the fields. She made a bee line to the migrant workers with cash andthey welcomed her opened legs with opened arms.

The men spent their left over earnings and free time 'inside' of Kathy's vagina. She had virtually moved into the cabin with the twenty or so men. They were allowed to run a tab in her and pay on Fridays. One was sent to buy drugs and beer for the weekend parties.

Kathy stayed with the 'Mexicans' for a week. Just as many ignorant people refer to all Orientals as Chinese, she referred to all the Hispanic men as Mexicans.

In fact, many of the men who traveled South picking crops were from South and Central America. North Americans had become far too uppity to pick the locals' crops, especially the cotton. You couldn't pay black folks to pick cotton in this day and age. Fuck that, wear some wool, nobody picking cotton. The foreigners were tough like that. They picked the cotton, strawberries and whatever else God pushed from the ground to feed mankind.

They did it for meager pay, most which went south to support their families. Kathy got what was left. Her vagina caliente and 'cerveza frio' were the main sources of entertainment.

Pedro Juan Salazar was the only one of the men who wouldn't touch the girl. He was a proud man, and he was disgusted by the loose young girl. Honor and dignity were high on his list of values. He had a wife and family waiting on him to collect enough money so he'd be able to send for them.

In his native country Columbia, Pedro was a soldier, a revolutionist. He was a leader of an insurgency against the tyrannical government, and as such, a target.

He fled in the middle of the night as the army forces swept down on his village. After a month of surviving in the jungle, he emerged tired, hungry and more determined than ever.

Pedro, along with a couple dozen men set out on foot in search of a better life for their families. Their destination was America, thousands of miles to the north. They walked, hitched rides on rail cars, and swam when necessary. By the time they'd reached Mexico, what started out as dozens, were now two. The rest had died trying.

His story, while interesting, is not the focus of the story. It just shows the determination and guts of his bloodline. He came from a long line of warriors and subsequently fathered one.

Pedro, almost always excused himself when the Kathy train was initiated. He would walk alone in the fields as the men took turns with the black whore.

It was sickness and fate that managed to get Pedro and Kathy alone. She felt so bad for him lying on his cot sick from fever, that she did her best to nurse him back to being healthy.

Pedro sipped the water she offered and thanked her with a weak smile. Kathy mistook the only semblance of friendship he'd ever offered to heart. His erection was hot from fever as she slid down onto it.

It only took a few rocks of her hips to get him to ejaculate inside of her. Just as he had survived the brutal trek from one continent to the next, it was his sperm that fought its way through the semen soup in the young whore's womb. It, out of the millions, found and burrowed inside of her just released egg.

Fate, it was fate that took Pedro in his sleep just as life was formed in Kathy. The migrant workers buried their comrade in a field set aside to plant the bodies of expendable workers.

A day later, a truck had come to escort them off to their next crop in the next state. A valiant protest to bring Kathy along fell on deaf ears. The sexual equivalent of a water boy was left behind.

****

"We gotta get that child some help," Mrs. Johnson whispered, as Kathy lay comatose on the sofa. It was needless to whisper because a marching band wouldn't wake the dead tired girl.

"I'm finna get her some help alright?" The deacon replied ominously.

"Who you calling?" His wife demanded, as he angrily dialed.

"Hey sheriff this is Deacon Johnson," he replied, answering the question and announcing his call. "Yes sir as a matter fact we have. She's here now."

Again, fate intervened and the 'Uncle Thom' deputy, Thom, answered the call. Deputy Mann wanted to take the call but was clear across the county. Good thing too, because she probably would have 'escaped' from Officer Mann,gotten lose, and ran off with a mouth full of "cum" if it were left to him.

"Guess I gotta give you the same thing I gave your lil buddy," the judge reckoned when Kathy was brought in front of him. "One year in state custody!"

The year-long sentence would mean the child she didn't know yet would be born into custody. At least it would be born. If left on the streets, it would have been aborted before she had ever known she was pregnant.

Of course, her popping up pregnant while incarcerated churned the rumor mill. Speculation ran wild as to who fathered the child. That was the question on Kathy's mind too.

With her being a ward of the state, the abortion she so desperately sought was beyond her reach. She, like everyone else would just have to wait until the child was born to start the second round of guessing.

When the extraordinarily pretty baby was finally born, Kathy was perplexed. She mentally ran the golden little face against the legions of men who stopped by to visit her vagina.

The baby's 'good hair' eliminated all of the nappy head locals and cleared most of the jail staff. She squinted and turned sideways at the baby trying to figure out who fathered it.

She surmised that it must have been put in her by one of the 'Mexicans'. The baby had a beautiful golden hue to its skin, hair and eyes; it had to have been conceived in the fields. The timing was right, so it just had to be.

"Tywanna," she smiled down naming the sleeping infant. She chose that name because it sounded Mexican to her. Mexican is of course, the language Mexicans speak.

Maybe if Kathy had gotten to spend more time with her baby, their story would have turned out to be different, but no such luck. This is Dope Girl and it's going to be gritty.

Deacon and Mrs. Johnson were of course on hand for the birth of their only grandchild. They were so upset and regretful at the outcome of their own child. This little baby represented another chance. Another shot to get it right.

They often wondered where they'd gone wrong with their daughter. It was often the subject of regret and remorse. The answer was nothing, they did nothing wrong. Society had touched their child and affected her more than they ever could have. It's hard for church to compete with the club.

Little Tywanna was taken to the Johnson home to begin her life, while her mother finished her bid.

Chapter 2

When a person's soul goes bad, it will desire what is harmful and takes pleasure in corruption, and will love it dearly. Kathy's soul had gone bad. She spent the rest of her time in jail planning on getting high.

She turned tricks with the guards and saved up her little change. Of course, no one would have actual intercourse with her after the pregnancy scares, but ten bucks would get your dick sucked. Kathy would hook you up through the cell bars if need be.

Over the next few months, Kathy sucked enough to put away money so that when she got out, she could hit the ground running. That's exactly what she did too, ran straight to the dope man. The trifling girl had to pass right by her house to get to the trap-house. She turned her head as the driver passed by to ease her guilty conscience; what was left of it anyway.

It was all good though, because young Tywanna was in good hands, great ones in fact, with her loving grandparents. Mr. and Mrs. Johnson doted on the sweet child.

Deacon was old school, a man's man. The biggest lesson he tactfully taught was what a man is. A man went to work every day to support his family. He did not curse, drink, or do drugs. He treated his woman like a queen and catered to her almost as much as she catered to him.

Her lesson was just as subtle, be a lady at all times. After all, how can you expect to be treated like a lady when you refuse to act like one? Most of what the young child was taught went over her head for the moment. They were life lessons which one would have to live to appreciate.

Still, it was like laying a concrete slab to build a house upon. No matter what life threw at her, from God's decree, she had a solid foundation to withstand the storms. A major storm was headed her way too, a shit storm.

"Are you ok Deacon?" Mrs. Johnson asked her distressed husband, who was struggling behind the wheel of their car.

"I... I...yes d-dear," he managed to reply, sugar coating the vice- like pain in his chest.

He was not ok. He was in the grip of a massive heart attack. Mr. Johnson tried his best to maintain the fast moving car. His last thoughts were of pulling off the road to ensure his family's safety, but unfortunately, he didn't make it.

"Deacon!" His wife yelled, as his head slumped down on his chest. Before she could stop the car, it drifted into the oncoming traffic. With her last bit of strength, she launched her frail frame into the backseat to cover her grandchild.

The move saved the girl's life but cost her grandmother hers. Her back was broken in the massive collision, but she refused to leave until her baby was safe. The responding rescue units had to use the 'jaws of life' to extricate the broken bodies from both of the crumpled cars.

It was only once Tywanna was free that Mrs. Johnson let go of this life. She cracked a weak smile and exhaled her soul so she could join her husband. She never did like for him to go anywhere without her. They had been close like that.

Young Tywanna was headed for state foster care once her mother was notified. When the crack whore was tracked down several weeks later, her reaction at the loss of her parents was, "ok."

She didn't even ask about her child. In her current state she barely remembered having one.

"They ain't have no insurance?" A fellow crack head asked as the bad news spread throughout the Trap house.

"Insurance?" Kathy asked curiously at the prospect of easy money.

Come to find out the Johnsons' did have insurance. Lots of it. Since Kathy never formally gave custody to her parents, the state couldn't prevent her from getting her now five year old child.

The insurance policy provided a monthly payment for the child's upbringing, as well as a lump sum payout when she turned 18. The house was hers as well.

"I'm yo' mama," Kathy said dryly when social workers brought Tywanna home.

"My mama dead!" Tywanna shot back bitterly.

"Lil' bitch I'm yo' damn mama! I'm the one who pushed your big ass head out of my pussy!"

"Um... Ms. Johnson? Let's go easy, she just went through a traumatic experience," the worker said attempting to soothe both mother and child.

Tywanna turned her nose up at the stranger and marched into her bedroom. Kathy 'hmpf-ed' and stomped off to her deceased parents' room that she had since commandeered.

Kathy tried at first, she really did. With the monthly checks, and food stamps she could make it. She was able to maintain for two whole days before her addiction got the best of her.

Having a house to smoke in was good for free get high. It wasn't long before half the junkies in Longs were hanging out at the Johnson house. What was once a good quiet Christian home was now turned out.

Kathy even let a small time dealer operate from her bedroom in exchange for keeping her pipe full. Tywanna was forced to her own bedroom to escape the strangers. Once the dealer moved on, Kathy returned to renting her body for dope.

The young girl was the unwilling witness of sex acts, long before her mind could process them. She wasn't quite sure what was going on, but the sights and sounds of it disgusted her.

Things took a turn for the worse when Kathy discovered that the monthly allotment of food stamps could be sold for crack. She would swipe her card in exchange for half of the total in cash. She got high but the cupboards ran dry.

Tywanna, just like the man she would one day call her father, had to learn at an early age how to fend for herself. At first, her hunger was easily satisfied by a visit to the tidy garden her grandfather kept out back. When it finally yielded its last, things became more challenging.

School offered breakfast and lunch, which on some days would have to suffice. A well timed tantrum in front of the right 'John' earned her a meal. Ironically, it was an ill-timed tantrum, in front of the wrong John, that opened a dark chapter in the young girl's life.

Kathy had tricked so much, for so long, that she had worn the elasticity out of her vagina. It was just about useless now. Likewise, poor dental care left ragged sharp edges around her teeth that could cut.

She was desperately trying to figure out a way to get a client off when Tywanna walked out and demanded to be fed. The John finally got an erection when the little girl came into view.

"Mama I'm hungry!" She protested keeping her eyes on the floor in front of her. The last time she pulled this stunt the trick threw her a few dollars just to get rid of her. This one wanted to pay for her to stay.

"Turn your back baby. I'll get you something in a few minutes. Just stay right there," Kathy pleaded as she stroked the man penis.

She had officially sold her child for sex. The pervert was able to get where he was trying to go just by looking at the child while Kathy touched him. The next time he came over he was more interested in the small child than the grown woman.

"Where's the girl?" He asked eagerly scanning the room.

"She's asleep," Kathy said firmly, hoping that would put an end to it.

"Well just let me look at her. Pull her gown up and let me see her. I'll pay you twenty dollars!" He said, stopping her head from shaking her head no. It now nodded yes.

It was a slow day in the middle of an even slower week, and she finally agreed.

Kathy turned her head as the predator stared down at her scrawny kid while pulling on himself. When he was ready to ejaculate he called Kathy over for use as a receptacle.

"Say Ah! Open wide!"

Chapter 3

Child molestation was the star of the next chapter in young Tywanna's life. There must be a pedophile grapevine, because soon, men were coming specifically to see the girl.

"Mama I'm not finna' let no man look at me!" Tywanna protested vehemently when her mother brought the plan to her.

It had gone against everything her real mama had taught her. Grandma said privates were private. That's why she had to sit with her legs closed and be modest.

"But baby, they gonna give us money to buy food," Kathy reasoned.

Some of the monsters would just masturbate while staring at the scrawny child. Kathy would blow a few others. It wasn't long before she relaxed the rules and allowed touching. Only problem was, Tywanna wasn't having it.

She employed a variety of techniques to combat being molested. At first, she did what any child would do; cry. Tywanna would pour her broken little heart out through her eyes anytime a man touched her. Sometimes it worked, other times not so much.

Some men would feel sorry for the bawling child and go home to their wives and children. Other men would only be more turned on by the crying.

The next tactic was playing skunk. She knew that the small mammal had no other defense than smelling bad. That's when she stopped bathing all together. She wouldn't wipe herself either after answering the call of nature.

The little girl stunk to high heaven and she could hardly stand it herself. As nasty as it was, it worked.

"That child might be dead in there!" One disgusted pedophile complained, as he rushed from the room. Can you imagine a pedophile disgusted by something?

"Wait! I'll bathe her!" Kathy called after him as he stormed out of the house.

Kathy came back into the house winded after chasing the car half a block. She was so mad she filled a bucket with hot sudsy water and washed her child in her bed.

"Think yo' ass is slick don't you!" She growled as she removed sweat and waste from her daughter. "Bet yo' 'lil ass be clean for the next one!"

When the next monster crawled from under his rock and came for a visit, she was indeed clean too. It was cool because Tywanna had another trick up her sleeve.

"Oh hell naw!" The child molester fumed as the little girl defecated on herself as soon as he touched her.

Tywanna couldn't help but laugh as she had chased yet another one off. That ploy worked well for a while, but some days when there was nothing to eat there was nothing to shit out.

Having run out of options, Tywanna began to fight the men. She had a decent hook game from fighting half of her school already. Playing skunk came at a cost and she was often teased. That was cool too because if you teased her, she would fight you, everyone except Big Bessie. Even the teachers let the oversized girl do whatever she wanted. Tywanna did her best to steer clear of Big Bessie.

The ferocious little fighter fought off every man that had entered her room. Most would leave when they couldn't get anywhere. Most that is, not all.

"Look baby, Mr. Grimes own that hotel, he got plenty money so please be nice to him," Kathy pleaded, as she introduced the elderly man.

Mr. Grimes was well into his sixties and still molesting kids. He started forty years back with his own kids, then their friends and eventually his own grandkids. He was as sick as they came.

Tywanna was almost hungry enough to go for it, almost but not quite. She lay there while the nasty old man rubbed her skinny legs. His hands felt like fire and burned into her flesh and soul.

When he attempted to touch her there, she snapped, and a hard kick sent his smile across the room as his dentures went flying. She jumped up and began wailing with everything she had.

It was a valiant effort but to no avail, she was no match for the grown man. He was a grown man who had no qualms about punching a little girl. The blow knocked the child out allowing him to have his way with her.

It could have been she could have been raped while she was unconscious and her mother oblivious. He tampered with her with his fingers and hands until she stirred awake. Once she awoke she fought again.

Her junky mother finally came in trailing crack exhaust and broke the fighting up. Mr. Grimes only paid half of the agreed upon fifty bucks, since the child was so much trouble.

That night was a turning point. Even Kathy was affected by the blood and the eye swollen shut. She gave her child a reprieve for as long as her habit would allow. It was over with though, the next time a man entered Tywanna's room he ran out leaking.

"What in the world?" Kathy said, as a bloody blur ran through the living room and out the front door. When she went into her daughter's room to investigate, what she saw frightened her to the core.

There was the little girl, holding a big knife, still dripping with the child molesters blood. It was over now. No more skunks, no more sleeping in the woods, no more being touched. It was over, next chapter.

Chapter 4

Middle school was just about as bad as Elementary for the social outcast. Tywanna didn't have many friends, but no real enemies either. She battled so many kids they either respected her, ignored her, or feared her. All except Big Bessie, who feared no man.

The man sized girl was as slow as she was big. Being a bully was the only thing in which she excelled. She terrorized the school and ruled with an iron fist; a big ham-hock sized iron fist.

No one was allowed to call her Big Bessie, just Bessie. A male teacher had made that mistake once, and she slapped him down. Of course, she was suspended for several weeks then allowed to return to her reign of terror. By far, her favorite target was Tywanna.

Tywanna didn't want to fight her, but wouldn't take her abuse either. Most kids ran, but she held her ground. All the bullies keep jesters and hype men at their sides, and Ema-mae was Big Bessie's.

Big Bessie got big and stayed big by eating other people's food. Every day in the school's cafeteria during breakfast and lunch, someone got jacked. She would eat an additional three, or four trays to augment her own.

This is where she and Tywanna butted heads. The girl was near starved and was not coming off her only meals. Bessie let it slide in favor of easier prey, but she was now on the girl's radar.

"Ooh, there she go Big Bes… I mean Bessie!"Ema-mae said, alerting her boss as Tywanna emerged from the school house.

She tried to stop short of adding the forbidden adjective to her name, but enough slipped out to get her slapped for it. It was only a tap, but it sent the smaller girl rolling in the dirt. She jumped up and dusted herself off as she rushed to catch up.

Big Bessie was marching towards Tywanna sending scared kids scrambling to get out of her way. They panicked upon seeing her, and sighed in relief once she had passed them by.

"I heard you had something to say 'bout me!" Bessie boomed down in her baritone voice. It was a lie of course but she needed an excuse to step to the girl.

Tywanna knew it as well but refused to back down. She was scared as any "David" would be when faced with a Goliath. Still she wouldn't cower or run.

"All I said was you're a big ugly cow!" Tywanna said fearlessly. The girl wanted trouble and she'd found it.

Bessie's big hand spread like a catcher's mitt and sped towards Tywanna's face before she could duck. The resulting smack sounded like thunder and made the side of her face go numb.

The heavy blow sent her staggering a few feet but she didn't fall. She bounced back wailing away with both fists. They traded blows at a twenty to one ratio until Big Bessie overwhelmed her with heavy blows.

Tywanna took a beating that day, and the next, and the one after that. She fought Big Bessie every day that the big girl tried her. She was content with losing fight after fight, but she was not giving up her food and she was not backing down. It sent a message to the other kids that spoke loud and clear. It may have gone on forever if Bessie hadn't crossed the line. She went too far and it was about to cost her.

"Eww! What is that?" Ema-mae said, reeling from the Mason jar filled with a murky brown liquid. It stunk right through the glass.

"Um, let's see," Bessie smiled. "A lil' pee, a lil' poop, um tobacco juice from grandma's spit jar, and spoiled milk."

"What you finna' do with that?" she replied in disgust. Who would make a concoction as vile as that and what could you possibly do with it. "Bout to give ole gal a drank," Bessie said, wickedly nodding towards Tywanna.

Ema-mae knew that was going too far but could only shake her head. Any protest might have earned a slap or worse yet, what was in the jar. The liquid seemed to be bubbling on its own as if it were fermenting.

Furthermore, she knew Tywanna had done nothing to deserve what was coming to her. The pretty, introvert girl kept to herself and minded her own business. She seemed totally unaffected or concerned with the goings on around her. But since she wasn't attached to any group or clique she was a target.

Well, perhaps target isn't the best term. Targets just stand there and take shots, Tywanna fought back. She returned fire when fired on.

As soon as she saw Bessie enter the cafeteria and scan the room she knew she was looking for her. She had just sat down with her breakfast tray and was desperately trying to eat before the inevitable fight.

"There she is," Bessie growled with a grin as she spotted Tywanna blowing on her hot grits. Ema-mae sadly fell in step behind her as she marched over.

Tywanna sensed the danger and alternated between looking at her and concentrating on her food. Last night there wasn't a scrap of food in the house, so this was it. Taking her eyes off the bully caused her to lose track of her progress.

The jar hissed loudly when Bessie un-capped it and began filling the room with funk. She was on top of the girl the next time she looked up.

"Here you go!" Bessie laughed as she tossed the disgusting cocktail in her face just as she put a spoonful of grits in her mouth.

The putrid fluid went into her eyes, nose and worse of all, her opened mouth. Only a small number of students actually laughed at the disgusting act. Most fumed in silence and sorrow for the victim. Most had themselves had been victims to Big Bessie a time or two.

Tywanna, meanwhile was in shock. The smell and taste was so offensive it took her breath away. Her clothes and hair rapidly soaked up the foul fluid.

Bessie braced herself for a fight but it never came. Instead, the unexpected happened and Tywanna began to cry. She broke down in sobs and heaves, at not only this act of abuse, but for all of them she had endured.

A shocked Big Bessie watched in wonderment as the ferocious fighter bawled. She turned away in satisfaction assuming she had broken the strong willed girl. Nothing could have been further away from the truth.

The truth was that while Tywanna spat the piss, shit and tobacco saliva from her mouth, she also made a vow. She was gonna kill Bessie, and soon.

Tywanna only owned two pairs of pants and three shirts. She walked briskly to her house hoping to bathe, change and get back to school before lunch. Lunch was the focus now that her breakfast had been spoiled, and chances were there would be no dinner.

When she rushed into her home there was Kathy doing what Kathy did most.

"GIRBAHJKNA!" she screamed, but a man's dick was too far down her throat to enunciate. She removed it from her tonsils before trying again. "Get out of here, you see mama's busy!"

It still took the stunned child a second to react. She had long seen her mother having sex with men, but this one had his thing in her mouth.

'Why in the world would he do that?' she wondered.

"Get out and take a bath you stink!" Kathy yelled alerting her to the fact that she hadn't moved.

With the house off limits Tywanna's only choice was the creek. There she could bathe and wash her clothes out. By the time she made it back to the school house her clothes would be dry courtesy of the hot Mississippi sun.

Tywanna scanned the area several times thoroughly before she stripped naked. Just as she began to wash her clothes, a man's voice called out behind her.

"Hey now, what we got here?" He asked drawing closer. "You Kathy's daughter, damn you got fine!"

Maurice remembered her from his visits to the house years earlier. He was one of the grown men who liked to masturbate while looking at a child. Nothing had changed and out came his penis.

"Just like old times," he cheered as he began to pull on himself.

Tywanna tried to retreat upstream but he followed her whooping and hollering the whole way. His intention was to humiliate her along with catching a nut.

The act was bad enough in itself, but the delay caused her to miss lunch as well. It would have been futile to try to sit in class with an empty stomach so she went home.

"Again?" Tywanna complained coming home to find yet another man humping Kathy's face. She turned on her heels quickly leaving her mother gagging on a stranger.

She ended up in her school away from school. The small town's small library taught her more than all of her teachers had combined. This is where she could be Cameisha the diva. She surfed, chatted and studied until the hunger pains could no longer be ignored. Luckily this was farm country, so food was plentiful. All she had to do was go pick some.

Chapter 5

The next day at school Big Bessie had virtually ignored Tywanna. When she didn't fight back she assumed she had conquered her and she moved on to the next victim. She had a jar of her foul brew fermenting at home for whoever else decided to say no to her.

No one did, most offered their food to her if she so much as glanced in their direction. Quite a few viewed Tywanna as a hero for standing up to the bully but their hopes died the day she didn't respond.

After an uneventful day at school Tywanna decided to stop by the local farms to collect her dinner. The lessons her grandmother had taught her prevented her from taking more than what she needed.

Now a vet, she knew what rows contained which vegetables. After gathering her dinner it was off to the pecan groves. A pocket full of nuts came in handy to chase back hunger.

When Tywanna ducked into a row of shady pecan trees, she heard the familiar sounds of sex wafting through the air. Curious and nosey, she crept forward to investigate.

"Take that, take that!" Maurice yelled, as he pounded a large female on all fours. The sounds of their skin slapping together echoed into the country air.

Tywanna couldn't see who the girl was so she quietly walked around to get a better view. She was shocked to see Big Bessie foraging for pecans while Maurice pumped for dear life. They were both trying to get a nut.

Maurice got his first and howled like an Indian in a cowboy movie, and then, he released inside the big girl who barely knew he was back there.

"Ooh wee!" Maurice sighed and tried to slump over on her back but she was ready to go.

"Let me have my money," she demanded, scrambling to her feet, and pulling her bloomers and jeans up, and on in one motion.

"Here you go gal. Five dollars!" he said, making it sound like more than it was. Five bucks wasn't much but it was plenty for what Bessie wanted.

"I'm finna' get me a fat-fat burger," she cheered holding the bill up like the Olympic torch.

A Ms. Anne fat-fat burger was indeed something to cheer about. It contained a half pound patty, deep fried in lard, sausage patties, bacon, ham, onions, bell peppers, mushrooms, four kinds of cheese and of course, special sauce.

It was legend in these parts. Poor Tywanna had longed to eat one but its five dollar price tag put it way out of her reach. The girl had yet to have two dollars at the same time, let alone five. The fat-fat burger was her holy grail.

"Meet me down by the creek tomorrow and we can go again," Maurice suggested as he finished dressing.

"Ok! And I can get me another fat-fat burger!" Bessie said doing the fat-fat dance.

The fact that the bully was gorging on fat-fat burgers while she was scrounging in fields like a rabbit, steamed Tywanna. She resolved to be down to the creek tomorrow too.

The next day, Tywanna watched Big Bessie pull off the same bloomers and jeans as the day before and lay down. Maurice too dropped the same clothes from the day before and took position between her legs.

Bessie played in the clovers and Maurice pounded away at her. He must not have been working with much because the girl hardly knew he was there.

"You like this? Tell me you like this!" He demanded as he thrust.

"Mm… hmm..I like it," Bessie replied dryly. She was actually talking about the rare four leaf clover she'd found. She held it up for inspection as he stroked away.

Maurice took two hard thrusts and grunted loud enough to evacuate all the birds from nearby trees. It also alerted Big Bessie that it was over and time to eat. She pushed the skinny man out of her and rushed to her feet. Using one hand to pull her clothes up she extended the other to get paid.

"I'ma have to take care of you on payday. I'm tight right now," he told her empty palm.

"Pay Day? I know you better pay me my money right now!" Bessie said confronting him.

"You better go on now gal! I ain't one of them kids you be bullying," he warned, adding a little extra bass to his voice.

"I want my money!" She screamed and shoved him. He shoved her back, and she took a swing at his face. Maurice ducked the slap but her finger nails grazed his face leaving four deep scratches in its wake.

"Oh hell naw!" Maurice whined as he lifted his hand to the missing skin. When he took a look at his bloody fingers his hand closed tightly into fist.

It took a couple of shots to knock the big girl on her big ass. Maurice knew her reputation for beating up men and got in the wind while she was dazed.

Bessie took to her feet, but was still woozy from the beating. One eye was swollen shut as she stumbled towards town. She was not going to make it.

Tywanna saw her chance for revenge and moved in to take it. She picked up a fallen tree limb and ducked behind a pecan tree. When the bully staggered past, she pounced.

The first blow with the branch sent bark flying, as it impacted with Bessie's head. It staggered the big girl again but didn't drop her. It was the next blow that knocked her out, and one or all of the next twenty that put her to sleep forever.

All that remained in Tywanna's hand when she finished was a bloody stump of branch. She knew the girl was dead but still leaned in to have a few words with her.

"Still like throwing pee on people? See where that got you, don't you?" She teased. "Oh that's right, dead people can't talk can they?"

When she finished her chat with the corpse she calmly collected her dinner and happily skipped home. Kathy was obviously attempting to set a record of some sorts, because Tywanna walked in to find yet another man's dick stuck in her head.

This time she would not be ran off. The days of running her off were down by the creek dead. Instead, she averted her eyes and went to her room to eat.

It took a day for Big Bessie's big corpse to be found. One more day before the skin under her finger nails and the semen in her body was matched to Maurice.

The sheriff joked that he put on an Oscar worthy performance in his claims of innocence. Of course, no one believed the registered sex offender, not with that much physical evidence.

When the case went to trial months later, it had only taken the jury five minutes to convict him. Actually, one minute. The other four were for coffee. Maurice was sentenced to die in the states death chamber. He was Tywanna's second body, but he would not be her last.

All the kid's from school came to Big Bessie's funeral, making her parents think she was well loved. She wasn't. People only came to see her in the casket. They wanted to make sure she was dead.

"Bye now," Tywanna whispered, fighting a smile as she filed past the cheap casket. "We'll holla."

Chapter 6

As bad as middle school was, high school was in some ways, worse. Considering that Tywanna had already once killed in middle school that was saying a lot. Kids didn't usually start killing each other until high school, unless you were in Chicago or the South Bronx, that is.

The first problem was puberty. Being malnourished as a child slowed her growth, but one morning, Tywanna woke up 'fine'. She desperately begged her breasts not to grow and tried to will her hips from spreading, but it was to no avail.

The extremely pretty girl was now a 'knock out'. Of course, that meant that none of her clothes fit anymore, and Kathy wasn't too big on school shopping.

"You can wear my clothes. We can share," Kathy offered at the dilemma.

"No thank you," Tywanna said politely to the Wilma Flintstone dress. That left only one option and it wasn't pretty.

"Oh no!" she groaned painfully as she inspected herself in her 'new' clothes.

Her new clothes were in fact, her grandmother's 'old' clothes. Even worse, they were old lady clothes. A good washing removed the moth ball smell but nothing could be done about the style. Straight color purple!

If one thing could be said in favor of the style-less dress it would be that it did conceal her shapely figure. While most of

Tywanna's classmates wore as little as they could get away with to show off their bodies, she tried her best to hide hers.

She knew getting teased was inevitable. The best she could hope for was someone showing up looking worse than her. Tywanna came up with a futile plan to wait until the bus was just about at the stop before making an appearance. This was to prevent being a sitting duck and the center of attention while they'd waited.

Tywanna boarded the crowded bus just before it pulled off. At first, it went eerily quiet, and then exploded into laughter.

"What in the world?" the teen bus driver exclaimed at the dated fashions.

"Ooh that's Mrs. Johnson's dress! My grandmamma made that!" A girl exclaimed as Tywanna sat down in front of her. For proof, she snatched the collar to show her grandmother's symbol.

"Get your hands off me!" Tywanna demanded shoving the girl's hand away. The teasing she could deal with, but there would be no touching. She had been touched enough in her short life. No more.

"Ooh!" The entire bus sang at the push, hoping to instigate a fight.

Anne wasn't much of a fighter but got caught up in all the pre-fight hype. Add that to the fact that half of the passengers on the bus were her cousins and she'd taken the bait.

"Don't be pushing my hand," she yelled and slapped the back of her head.

Some lessons in life are learned harder than others. This was going to be one of the hard ones. The moral of the short, but brutal message was that you do not slap a puncher.

The fight was over before it really began. Tywanna spun around and got on Anne's ass before her cousins could blink. The bus was completely silent except for the 'pap-pap' sound of flurried blows. In an instant, the pretty girl was made ugly. Her entire face was completely covered with knots, lumps and welts.

When Anne finally escaped the onslaught by diving under the bus bench, the girl's cousins moved in.

Tywanna took a beating, but dished out enough punishment to make the girls think twice about fucking with her again. They deliberately scratched her pretty face and tugged at her good hair.

Luckily for Tywanna applications of cocoa butter along with the generous Mississippi sun healed the scratches completely. In a week she was pretty as ever and the girls teased from a distance. There was no more touching, from the girls any way. In a month's time she had fought half the school. Some she'd won, some she'd lost. But since even the ones who managed to beat her didn't want to tangle with her again, you could put those down as a win too.

The old lady clothes regulated the boys to glance at her pretty face then they moved their vision to the half-naked girls. Tywanna was near invisible until gym class, that is.

One word had gotten out about how fine she was in the little school issued shorts and the guys flocked to see firsthand. Since seeing wasn't enough, some of the more "manish" boys groped and copped feels. Of course, she fought each and every one of them who did. She had a rule: grab a breast get a knot on your head.

Some of the teachers had taken up issues with Tywanna as well because she often corrected their misinformation. She was smart enough to research and verify everything they taught. The information she was able to gather was far better than what was contained in the antiquated books the school refused to update and replace.

School did have two pluses, breakfast and lunch. The steaming bowl of grits, eggs and biscuit filled her grumbling tummy. Lunch was usually peanut butter and jelly, milk and apple sauce. Sometimes it would have to last until breakfast rolled around the next day.

The more fortunate students packed their own lunches. They would heat their fat-fat burgers in the microwave filling the cafeteria with fat-fat aroma. Of course, they had to make a big show of eating a fat-fat burger. Some would do the fat-fat dance before sitting down to eat on it.

Then 'mmm' loudly upon the first bite as fat-fat juice ran down their arms. Tywanna could only watch lustfully as kids ate the fabled burger that was beyond her reach. She vowed to one day get one of her own and do the fat-fat dance.

Chapter 7

Tywanna constantly challenging her teachers finally landed her in hot water. They took their claims of her 'sassing' them to the principal who called her to the office.

"Gal, you can't keep mouthing off in class," he began. "They tell me you getting 'worser' by the day!"

"Worser, sir I'm getting worse," she corrected stifling a smirk.

"Excuse me? You think this is funny?" He barked.

"No sir, just worser ain't a word. I'm worse," she laughed. When the principal's pink face grew beet red she really cracked up.

"You get your ass out of here! You're suspended. I will be calling your mama!" He yelled rising to his feet and pointing at the door.

The threat to call her mother made Tywanna laugh even harder as she left the office and the school. Unless he had the number to the crack house, he wouldn't be calling her mother, who wouldn't care anyway. If it couldn't be put on the end of her pipe and smoked, Kathy was not interested.

The vacation meant Tywanna could spend her time where she wanted to be anyway. She merely existed in the real world; it was cyber space where she could 'live'. There she was Cameisha, the popular girl, outgoing, funny and even a little flirty.

There she chatted and gossiped with her friends from all over the world about factors of life she had yet to experience.

The library would close long before she got her fill, but she was forced to leave.

It was only then that her empty stomach became noticeable. The local farms had given up all they could for the season which meant she would have to find a different route. She headed into town to see what she could forage. The elation of the day's travels was visible on her pretty face as she practically skipped to town.

That's how Emit saw her for the first time. His car swerved when he first laid eyes on the pretty young thing. That's exactly what he was in the market for.

The recently widowed steel worker was comfortably middle class. He owned his own land and house in a neighboring county. Emit was hands down the most eligible bachelor in five counties.

Even at his wife's funeral, women, including her closest friends, shamelessly threw themselves at him. They weren't there to see her off, but to try and replace her.

Only problem was, Emit wanted something young. Something fresh and moldable to shape to fit him. None of the jilted mothers would sign the license allowing him take their daughters as a wife. Even when he offered cold cash he was denied. Pride cost more than money around these parts.

News of the crack head in Longs with the gorgeous daughter reached him so he came to town to investigate. He could only wish that the pretty girl he spotted on his way to Kathy's house was actually her. She certainly fit the description.

Emit found the now decrepit Johnson home and pulled to a stop. The creaky stairs threatened to give way under his weight as he approached the door. He knocked and posted a smile on his face as he waited.

"'cuse me ma'am," he began, ever the gentleman complete with a bow and tip of the hat. When he glanced up at the ravaged little crack head he almost turned on his heels.

"Ten for head, and twenty if you wanna fuck," Kathy said explaining the menu. "But since I got my period you can fuck for ten."

It took Emit, who had never come across a crack whore, a minute to process what the odd little woman was saying. He frowned and shook his head in disgust once he got it.

"Do you have a daughter? I was told you have a daughter," he said impatiently. Giving a glimpse of the dangerous personality that lay under the surface of the nice guy façade.

"Yeah but she a good girl. She ain't gone do nothing," Kathy said bitterly even though she should have been proud. Half the girls her age were already fucking and half of them had babies. Instead, she was mad because her daughter was chaste.

"Well that's good to hear," Emit proclaimed. Out of the young girls he was able to get parental permission for, they were all fast ass little girls. Some had a baby or two already. "I'm looking to marry."

"Marry?" Kathy laughed. "Tywanna ain't but…Twel? No she…is…um fourteen? No, Fifteen!"

"Old enough!" Emit cheered. "Law says as long as the parent signs we can get married. And, I'll pay you a dowry!"

"What the hell I'm gonna do with some seasoning salt?" Kathy frowned. She hadn't cooked a meal in years and smoked more than she ate.

"Not Lowery's! A dowry. A bride price. I'll give you five thousand dollars!" He said, hoping the daughter was as dumb as the mother. The dumb ones are easier to train. The thought of a young pretty and stupid girl almost gave him an erection.

"Ten thousand!" Kathy shot back quickly. Even a rural Mississippi crack addict knew people always offered half of what they were really willing to pay.

"You want me to sign my daughter over to you, then you gotta give me ten thousand dollars!" she proclaimed triumphantly.

Emit started to open his mouth to haggle a bit but the front door opened first. When Tywanna saw the man she instinctively ducked her head and quickened the pace to her bedroom sanctuary.

The couple of seconds Emit had seen her killed all negotiations. He was just relieved the crack addict didn't say twenty grand because he would have paid it. Luckily, her little mind didn't think that high.

The rumors didn't do her justice, Tywanna wasn't pretty, she was gorgeous. Even the old lady dress she wore couldn't fully conceal the curves on the child. The way that dress was poking out in the back bore witness that she was working with a lil' something.

"Ten it is!" he said, as if he were in an auction. In a way he was, since he'd just bought a person. "I'll come by tomorrow with the cash and we can head over to the courthouse and handle the paperwork."

"Well, how much you got on you now?" Kathy asked shamelessly. She had that money spent already.

"Guess I can stand to part with a few dollars." Emit sighed. He reached into his pocket and removed a sizable bankroll and peeled off two twenties. "I'll be round 'bout two tomorrow."

Times were slow and in the bad economy forty bucks equaled four sucked dicks. It was enough to buy a meal for her child and get a couple of rocks. She could finally get one of those fat-fat burgers she was always going on and on about.

As soon as the money touched her desperate palm it chased all thoughts of anything but getting high far, far way. Besides, her daughter would be fine. She hadn't fed the girl in months and she'd managed.

Tywanna heard the man leave and assumed he must have left some money behind with his semen. If she caught her mother before she got that pipe in her mouth she had a shot at a meal.

"Mama?" she called out as she ventured into the empty living room. A check of her empty bedroom confirmed Kathy was in the wind. Kathy beat him down the steps as she rushed over to the trap house.

More out of habit than actual success, Tywanna went to check the fridge. She could still remember vividly when it was stocked with food. Fresh fruits and vegetables, and pots full of delicious leftovers cooked by her grandmother. Now all it contained was a long ago burned out bulb.

"And 'I'm the lil' bitch?" she asked angrily and slammed the door. It was the closest she ever came to talking back. She would give her sorry mother an earful whenever she was out of ear shot.

As unfit as her mother was she still respected her. It was one of the lessons taught by her loving grandmother; lessons that were etched in stone.

Since the gardens were out Tywanna opted for plan B. The supermarket. She wouldn't steal because she was raised better than that. Luckily she wouldn't have to.

Most people in town knew her plight including the clerks at the market. They generously allowed her to keep her dignity by offering free samples of different foods. They made sure to pile it on so she could get full.

The only downside to the market was having to past right by the Fat-Fat Burger Shop. Tywanna crossed the street as she neared hoping to put a little distance between herself and what she couldn't have. It was futile though because fat-fat burgers had an aroma that traveled for miles. The smell was so strong you could taste it.

Dinner was several pieces of a new sausage the store grilled for customers to sample. The lady in the deli asked Tywanna to try the new cheese and the man in the bakery needed her opinion on a batch of fresh baked muffins. Water from the fountain washed it all down and sent the girl home full. Mission accomplished.

Chapter 8

"I need you to come straight home from school today," Kathy advised as Tywanna prepared to leave. "That man who was here yesterday wants to talk to you about something."

"Ok mama," Tywanna said, while simultaneously saying 'yeah right' inside her head. Anything a friend of hers had to say, she was sure she didn't need to hear.

It still amazed the girl how many handsome and well to do men would come by to see her mother. She knew a lot of them had wives and families, so why Kathy?

"Probably cuz she let them put they thang in her mouth," she assumed bitterly. She assumed right too because that's exactly why they came.

Kathy had lost all of her teeth by now and had a mean head game. All gums and tongue, just the way they liked it. Men of all incomes and social levels would pop in to get their dicks sucked. A good blow job could lessen the severity of whatever the day may bring. A ray of sunshine, a breath of fresh air. Head, it does a body good!

She had long ago traded her looks for dope. Her once fine frame was ashy skin and frail bone. Even the once luxurious head of shiny black thick hair was gone. Kathy now looked like she had an angry cat atop her head.

"Shit!" Tywanna cursed seeing the same fancy car sitting in front of the house when she came from school. If she hadn't forgotten her library card she would have went straight there, for some reason the old librarian insisted on checking it every day even though she was sometimes the only visitor all day.

"Here she is!" Kathy sang so cheerfully Tywanna became weary.

Emit smiled so brightly it only made her more uncomfortable. It reminded her of when she was young and helpless, too little to fight back.

"Hey little lady," he said, tipping his hat to her. Tywanna just stared back without responding. "Shy, that's good."

"This is the man I told you about. Are you still ok with what we talked about?" Kathy asked double talking them both.

"Um, yeah mama. Soon as I get back. I just gotta run out for a sec," Tywanna rambled and rushed to her room. She grabbed her passport to the outside world and rushed back out. The plan was to go wait out whatever her conniving mother had working in that devious head of hers.

"See, I told you!" Kathy lied. She produced the marriage consent form with one hand and an opened palm. "Where's my money!"

"Here you go," Emit said, snatching the paper just as eagerly as she'd snatched the cash filled bank envelope.

Once the swap was made they began to wait, and wait, then wait some more.

"What time you reckon that gal will be back?" Emit asked growing impatient. The justice of the peace would be closed soon ruining his plans for the evening.

He wanted to rush her over there and exchange vows so he could get her home and put his dick in her. Emit barely slept a wink anticipating getting his big paws on the girl.

"She's young, probably out gallivanting with her friends. Want me to suck yo' thang while we wait?" Kathy asked ever the good host.

"Just assume suck it myself 'fo I put it in that mouth of yours," Emit spat repulsed. He was growing agitated and impatient, but he wasn't the only one.

The little addict who hadn't had a blast all day now had ten thousand smokable dollars. It was pure torture for her.

"Why don't you swing by the library on Maple and give her a ride back," Kathy advised. She needed him to give her enough time to smoke a rock or two. If he would have blinked she would have left.

"I'll be right back then," he said taking to his feet. "If she ain't there we gone have a problem. I want my wife or my money back."

Tywanna had used the well-worn path through the woods and emerged just as Emit pulled off. She smiled assuming the ordeal was over and went inside. Nothing could have been further from the truth. In fact, the ordeal had just begun. Kathy hadn't left yet so she took a shot at trying to explain.

"I ain't finna' marry that man!" Tywanna protested "I don't even know his name."

"Emit," Kathy shot back as if that settled it. "You ain't even really got to go through with it. Just ride down to the court house with him."

Kathy knew her child and knew she wasn't hearing 'nare day of marrying the stranger. There was no way she was giving a coin of that money back either.

"Ok mama, let me go change," Tywanna lied.

"Me too," Kathy lied back. Good thing their rooms were on opposite sides of the house, because they both entered their rooms, closed the doors, and went out the window.

They both set off in different directions, toward different fates. For Kathy, her first stop was to the trap house. She spent a hundred dollars on what would be a twenty anywhere else in the country.

The local junkies who had visited or lived in other cities often told tales of humungous rocks that smoked for hours. It was like fishermen tales for crack heads. Far away magical lands with dimes the size of softballs.

When Kathy blazed through the paltry amount, she made the decision to take her show on the road. At the rate she smoked the tiny rocks, she would be broke in a week and of course there was still Emit.

She gave a quick blow job in exchange for a ride to the bus station. Armed with enough money to buy clothes in her cheap purse, she had no need to stop by the house.

"When is the next bus?" She inquired looking up at the schedule for the proverbial first thing smoking.

"Ten minutes," the clerk replied.

"How much?" Kathy asked not caring where the bus was heading. It really didn't matter as long as it was away from Longs Mississippi.

"Dallas Texas, eighty nine dollars please."

"Keep the change." The big spender said handing over one of the crisp hundred dollar bills. She spent five of the ten minute wait smoking the residue from her shooter.

Kathy stared out into the blackness as the bus sped along the highway. Her thoughts bounced from this to that never once landing on her child. She deserved what was about to happen to her.

Most bus terminals are shady, shadowy places where criminals and chicken hawks search for prey. Pimps patrol them in search of run-aways to turn out. Dope, death and deception are always nearby.

Dallas was one of the few exceptions. The extremely busy terminal was set in the heart of downtown, meaning you had to go looking for trouble.

"M.L.K," Kathy announced hopping in the back of a taxi in search of trouble.

Every major city in America has a Martin Luther King Blvd and it's always dead in the hood. No matter what state, if you want some dope or pussy M.L.K. was the place to be. The slain civil rights Icon is probably turning over in his grave.

A short cab ride later they hit M.L.K. and a shabby motel caught her eye. The amount of obvious junkies milling about suggested a vibrant drug trade and caused Kathy's stomach to churn.

"Right here!"She cheered as triumphantly as a mountain climber reaching an apex.

She was famished from the long ride but decided to grab a room and a quick blast. She would sit down and eat afterwards. Yeah, right! That first hit would run hunger off in an instant.

After checking out the drab room that would be her new home for the rest of her life, Kathy set out in search of rocks.

"Cuse me," she said calling the first junky she saw outside of her room. "I'll buy if you fly."

"Hell yeah!!" The addict replied and rushed over to the room. "My name Lady."

"Kathy," Kathy replied as she opened her purse to retrieve some money. The tramp known as Lady passed gas loudly at the sight of all the hundred dollar bills.

"You must not be from 'round here,'" Lady commented at the stupidity of pulling out a wad of cash in front of a stranger.

You could do that back in Longs Mississippi, but this was Dallas Texas, and this particular crack whore was particularly treacherous.

"No ma'am. I'm from Mississippi," Kathy said proudly.

"Well, I ain't tryna get in yo' business," Lady said, which is what people say right before they get in your business, "but um, you should hide some of that money. Don't keep it all in one place."

"You think so?" Kathy asked naively, and then answered; "you right, 'cause ten thousand is a lot of money!"

Lady passed gas again upon hearing the amount. Ten grand would keep her high off crack and drunk off cheap liquor for months.

"Put half, no put all but a couple of hundred under the bed," Lady said lifting the box spring off of the wood frame. The compartment was large enough to stash a body and had been used for just that on several occasions.

"OK, I'ma keep out five hundred and hide the rest." Kathy agreed. She counted out five bills and dropped the rest under the bed.

"I'll be right back," Lady said taking off with one of the hundreds. She recruited a junky/dealer who was perfect for what she had in mind.

"Kathy, this is Gerrald. Gerrald, Kathy," she said, formally introducing the two when she returned.

"Hey Gerrald," Kathy said cheerfully then showed him her gums. It was her turn to pass gas now once she saw how much crack a hundred dollars bought in Dallas.

She didn't see anything else as she scrambled to get a piece of that rock into her pipe. She hadn't seen Gerrald sneak behind her. Just as she lit the lighter in an attempt to take a long overdue blast, Gerrald put her in a choke hold. It was text book perfect and would have made L.A.P.D proud.

When the pressure hit her wind pipe the crack pipe went one way and the lighter went another. Kathy was more concerned with reaching for the dope than the death grip on her throat.

Lady quickly scooped them up and took a long hit. Dying must suck, but dying while watching someone smoke your rocks must really sting. Talk about adding insult to injury.

She blew a long steam of crack exhaust out just as Gerrald let Kathy's new corpse fall to the filthy floor. Lady snatched up her purse and rummaged inside.

"Here go the mo…," was all she got out before Gerrald hit her with a Teddy Pendergrass uppercut that turned off her lights.

Lady woke up twenty minutes later, face to face with Kathy on the floor. The sturdy crack whore had been knocked out plenty of times in her career and had shaken it off. Crackheads are as tough as Tonka trucks.

"Never trust a crack head," she told Kathy as she climbed to her feet. Lady went under the box spring and collected the bulk of the money.

"And, I'm calling the police," she chuckled at the thought of the two thousand dollar 'crime stoppers' reward she could claim for reporting the murder.

No, never trust a crack head. Indeed.

Chapter 9

When Tywanna's feet landed outside of her window she too headed for the bus depot. Only this one was where the school buses were parked. She traveled to the back of the lot where the older buses that were no longer in service were parked.

She had her own bus that served as a home away from home. This is where she would retreat to escape the flow of child molesters her mother brought home. The bus had been cleaned and made tidy for overnight visits.

The long day had taken its toll on the young girl and she was asleep soon after arriving. In the deep sleep the night passed in minutes. A glance at her cheap watch confirmed why her belly was grumbling, she had missed breakfast at school.

Since school without breakfast was futile she decided to skip for the day. After foraging for food out of the local gardens and groves, Tywanna headed to the higher learning the internet had to offer. It would be good to get out of Longs Mississippi for the day. Little did she know it would be her last day here for many years to come.

At the same time Emit was turning the small town upside down in search of the two women. Now he was convinced he had been swindled and was none too happy. He had spent the night parked in front of the empty Johnson house waiting on his prey.

When his temper reached a boiling point he marched up the steps and through the front door. Had he not been such a brute he would have seen the door was unlocked. Instead he used his broad shoulder to reduce it to splinters. A quick search of the small house told him no one was there. The open bedroom windows proved he got tricked out of his money.

It only took a few inquiries in the tiny town, where everyone minded everyone else's business, to get the news that Kathy fled town. That meant quite a few dicks would go un-sucked. The news of her death would never make it back to Longs. She was going to be one of those 'what ever happened to' people.

When her unidentified corpse was found a day later, she was buried in a cardboard box in Potter's Field, laid to rest with the homeless and thrown away people. Her cheap headstone read Jane Doe #5312. It should have read Karma.

"I'm looking for my wife!" Emit demanded when he barged into the small school.

"Does she work here?" A frightened employee asked.

"Tywanna Johnson! I paid for her, where's she at?" He yelled. "Bring her to me now!"

"She's not in school today," the office worker replied.

Emit didn't take her word for it and began a room by classroom search. He barged into every class and demanded his bride. He waved his worthless marital consent form around to prove his claim. When he reached the room Tywanna would have been in had she come to school, he finally got some information on her whereabouts.

"She's over to the ..... What you call that place? The place that got all 'dem books?" A goofy class mate snitched. Silly girl knew every word to every new song minutes after it came out but couldn't even say library.

"The library!" Another student cheered, taking a guess. She had never actually been there herself but at least knew the name.

As Tywanna surfed, chatted and liked online, the man who would change her life came swaggering in. He glanced around dangerously and made eye contact. She quickly averted her eyes from the gorgeous stranger.

He came over and took the computer next to her and began his search, a search made dreadfully tedious by the antique dial up modem attached to the dated computers. Tywanna stole glances at him while he worked.

"Shit, shit, shit," Cam growled as his search repeatedly yielded the same results. Every time he entered his name in, the only thing that came up was wanted posters of him and news of the recent shoot out. A glance over at the cute little girl next to him proved she knew what she was doing.

"Say Shawty, how you goggle a nigga?"he said, purposefully mispronouncing the word to break the ice.

"You mean google!" Tywanna replied laughing, lighting up the drab room with her smile. "Does he have a Facebook? That's probably the quickest way to find someone."

"A what?" Cam asked curiously. Of course, he had heard of the social media giant, but real Dope Boys Did Not maintain an online presence. Note to all the "fronters".

"What's his name?" She asked as she switched screens to her account. She caught her own flirtatious tone and realized she was still in her online persona Cameisha.

"Cameron Forrest, F.o.r.r.e.s.t." He replied spelling needlessly as she had it searching before he finished.

"You hafta' buy me lunch for helping you," Cameisha demanded. Tywanna was so happy Cameisha was here, she never would have been brave enough to ask.

"That's what's up, lil' mama." He agreed standing to look over her shoulder. Cam wrinkled his nose at the slight odor emanating from the pretty little girl. Cute but stinks, he thought to himself.

"Wow! It's a lot of them. What state does he live in?" she asked to narrow the parameters.

"New York. Check for New York City," he replied looking at the results. Cameron Forrest was obviously a popular white guy name because the screen was full of them.

"New York City," she repeated as she typed and hit enter. "Here you go."

Cameron Forrest Junior took a deep breath as an older version of his own face appeared on the screen. The similarity was so striking even Tywanna immediately clicked on his profile.

"I may be dying, but so are you. Life in itself is a terminal demesne," Tywanna said reading the latest post. "It's from a few minutes ago!"

"That's him," Cam croaked a he stared at the father he'd never met.

"I'll send him a message, give me your number?" Tywanna asked as she typed.

"Shit! I ain't got a phone," he fumed. Cam had wisely tossed his phone out the window after the shootout. It would not be used as a tracking device against him. "Tell him it's his son Cameron, give your number."

"Ok, but you gonna hafta' put some minutes on it," Tywanna agreed. The cheap little phone was left behind as payment for Kathy, who accepted payment in kind as well as in cash. If you didn't have money for a blow job she would accept trinkets and small appliances.

"No problem." Cam huffed like it was a problem.

"Minutes and a fat-fat burger!" Tywanna cheered. This was shaping up to be her best day ever. She'd never had minutes on the phone and a Fat-Fat burger!

"A what?" Cameron laughed at both the strange name and the young girl's sudden enthusiasm. She was practically bouncing in the chair.

"A fat-fat burger! It's got meat and cheese and onions and...."

"Ok, ok, yeah you can have your fat-fat burger." He cut in ending the lengthy ingredient list. In fact he had heard enough to want a fat-fat burger himself.

"You got a deal shawty, what's your name?" He laughed.

"Tywanna!" she blurted out before she had the chance to lie. She would have preferred to be Cameisha for the man. "What's yours?"

"Um, Mike," he replied forgetting he had already told her his real name. "Come on so we can get our big fat burgers"

"Fat-fat burger!" She corrected doing a mobile version of the fat-fat dance as she led the way outside.

"There your little ass is! Brang yo ass over here right now!" Emit demanded as he pulled up. He was so thirsty he hadn't even stopped his car completely. It rolled to a stop against the building as he rushed over to Tywanna.

"Um, uh! I ain't going nowhere with you Willie!" Tywanna yelled as she took cover behind Cam.

Cam could only shake his head at his luck. Here he was a national fugitive on the run, about to get jammed up in a domestic dispute. He could only assume the older man was her father and knew he had to tread lightly. He couldn't interfere but he needed to get that call.

"Excuse me. I don't mean to get in your business Mr. Willie, but I…"

"My name ain't no damn Willie and you best stay out my business!" He shot back. "Now I done paid good money for this gal, she coming with me!"

"You can't make me marry you mista'!" Tywanna screamed. The situation was getting out of hand quickly as tempers flared.

"Paid for her?" Cam asked now getting heated himself. He may be a drug dealer and killer, but kids were off limits. Still he calmly approached the man hoping to quickly resolve the issue.

"Look, why don't I…"

Emit slapped the rest of whatever he was about to say over to the neighboring county. Cam instinctively reached to his waist, where a gun would usually be found, but came up empty.

Instead of killing the man Cameron tossed a two piece combo at him that would have made Mike Tyson proud. The left, right to the big man's chin dropped him to his knees. He was in perfect position for the kick that put him to sleep.

"Fuck!" Cam cursed at the commotion. "What the hell was that all about?"

He rushed to his car with the girl hot on his heels. She was in and seated before he was. He decided he would give her a couple bucks for the phone and her food and put her out a block away. Until she answered that is.

"My junky mama tried to sell me to that man." She replied bitterly.

The reply touched Cam but what could he do? He was running for his life, he didn't need any extra weight. Yeah she could get a few bucks but she had to go.

As Cam pulled into the motel he saw the creepy old clerk peep through the blinds. He ducked away when he turned his head in that direction. The move spooked Cam and confirmed what he already knew; it was time to move on.

"Say shawty, walk over to that burger joint and grab our food," Cam ordered once they entered his hotel room.

He opened his bag and removed one of the crisp hundred dollar bills. Tywanna frowned at the gun, the money and the suggestion.

"Walk! That's too far!" she protested. "And that man out there!"

"Leave the phone here, and grab me a sweet tea too," he said ignoring her protest. He grabbed a few items and went to take a quick shower before he got on the road. He planned to be gone by the time she returned.

Cam jumped in the shower when he heard the door open and close. It opened again and closed once again a minute later. Tywanna had come back for the big gun for protection. She admired the bundles of cash that was more money than she'd ever seen in her short life.

Route six ran parallel to route five where the fat-fat burger was made. Tywanna took a deep breath and cut through the woods. She actually felt safer there than on the streets where an angry steel worker was searching for her. The short cut shaved enough time off the trip to change history.

"I know this lil' girl ain't back already!" Cam sighed. He wrapped the towel around his waist and rushed out to dismiss the kid once and for all. "Look here lil mama, I..."

"I know you boy. Seen ya' on da news," the motel clerk snarled. He had what appeared to be the biggest shot gun ever made leveled at Cam's mid-section. A tug on the trigger would have cut him in half.

"There's money on yo' head boy," the clerk advised, explaining his presence.

"I got money too! Right there in that bag like thirty thousand," Cameron urged hoping to buy his way out of the situation.

He was fully prepared to pay his last cent to remain free if that's what it took. Poor and free, beat the hell out of being rich and in jail.

"I reckon I'll take that money there and still claim the reward 'fo turning ya' in!" The greedy man announced. To Cam it sounded like "please take this shot gun from me, ram it up my ass and blow my head off." He planned to do just that.

"Just look at, count it. It may be more like a hundred grand. Dump it out on the bed and look," Cam said. He planned to make play for his gun as it hit the bed. His muscles tensed as he prepared to leap, but the gun was gone.

"Shut my mouth!" The clerk exclaimed at the sight of all that cash.

Cam was perplexed as to what happened to his gun until the partially open door began to ease open.

"Put it down mister!" Tywanna demanded with Cam's gun pointed at him, a greasy bag full of fat-fat burgers and fixings clutched tightly in the other hand.

Her eyes grew large with fear when the man turned to face her. It was old man Grimes, the one who molested her as a child.

"Put that gun down gal!" He demanded so forcefully she started to comply. Then her face changed into a mask of fury.

Cam was set to make his move but the girl lifted his gun and fired. The slug tore into old man Grimes' forehead and out of the top of his skull. A piece of scalp with fuzzy grey hair was stuck on the ceiling.

It had taken a split second for Cam who was frozen in place from shock to react. Clad only in the towel, he scooped his money back in the bag and dashed out the door.

Again, Tywanna was seated in the care before him. He shook off the thought of putting her out as he pulled away from the murder scene. She had just saved his ass, he owed her.

"Is that man dead?" Tywanna asked solemnly as they sped away. Cam cast her an incredulous glance when she asked. Surely she saw his head explode.

"Yes, yes he is," he answered honestly and soothingly. He was prepared to try to comfort her, but she started laughing hysterically.

"Yesss!" she cheered pumping her little fist. It was pretty much the same reaction she had when the news of Big Bessie's death swept through the school. When the realization that she'd caused the death hit home, she shrugged an "oh well" shrug and went on with her life;life is after all for the living.

"Oh No!" she suddenly moaned and switched gears. Now the girl was crying her little eyes out just as hard as she had been laughing only seconds ago.

"You had no choice shawty. It was him or us. He would have killed us," Cam offered.

"That's not why I'm crying! To hell with that man. He molested me," she finally admitted.

"Shit, why you crying then?"

"Cause! I dropped the fat-fat burger!" she yelled painfully before launching into another round of crying.

Cam felt so bad for her that the thought of going back crossed his mind. He knew that motel was a full crime scene by now; a crime scene with his name written all over it. He was already hot when he left Atlanta, now he was a man on fire.

"We finna' go to New York?" Tywanna asked. The smart girl knew 'he' was now a 'we', because she wasn't going anywhere.

"Yeah lil mama, 'we' finna' go to New York."

Chapter 10

The girl was still crying halfway through Alabama, and Cam knew it was something other than not eating a burger that was eating away at her. He waited until the sobs let up before finding out what was bothering her to the point of tears.

"Lil mama we can find another spot that makes the fat-fat burgers," he offered trying to do the fat-fat dance himself. He failed miserably, but managed to get a smile on her tear slicked face.

"Just thinking 'bout my mama," she sighed. Tywanna knew she would never see her mother again, not in this life anyway.

Even though Kathy was unfit and never did anything for the girl, she still loved her. That set off another round of tears, but she was still able to speak.

"My mama sold me. Sold me!" she said trying to come to terms with it.

"Where's your daddy?" Cam inquired in hopes for someone or somewhere to leave the kid.

"Hmpf, what's that?" Tywanna huffed. "I ain't never met or heard nothing 'bout him. My grandma said I'm part Mexican or something."

"Well, I'm you're your daddy now," Cam vowed. He was taking responsibility for the girl who had saved his ass.

Cam pulled over just before the Georgia line and replaced the girl's phone that they'd hurriedly left at the motel. He also needed to build his courage up before entering the state that wanted to kill him. If he could have driven around it, instead of through it, he would have. But, that was not an option.

Tywanna went online and sent another message to Cameron Forrest senior. Minutes later just as they entered the state of Georgia, the phone rang. "212 must be for your daddy," Tywanna beamed. It was the first time she had a chance to use the word and it felt good.

"Hold on," Cam said upon answering and dangerously pulled off the highway and onto the shoulder.

"A-yo, who's dis?" The deep voice on the other end boomed, when Cam came back on the line.

"Cameron, this is Cameron Forrest," Cam said defiantly. "Your son."

"My what! Nigga find something safer to play with!" Senior barked and hung up.

Cam was steaming at the snub. While hitting redial, he pressed the send button so hard, the cheap phone threatened to break.

"Check this shawty! I do got a million things better to do then to call niggas talking about they're my daddy!" Cam barked. "You remember Tywanna? My momma, from Atlanta?"

"Eastwyck in Decatur?" His father asked after a protracted silence. "Yeah I know, well, knew her, so what?"

"She named me after my father, you!"

"Damn!" Cameron senior sighed as memories came rushing back. He had been in love with the young girl who was in love with the streets.

Senior remembered hearing that she was pregnant but he was already back in New York by then. Given the girls promiscuity, there was no way for him to know he was the father. But still?

"Aight, so why you just now getting at me? What do you want?" He asked skeptically. "Where are you?"

"I'm on 75 north headed your way and I'm hot as hell!" Cam replied.

"Hot huh? Must be my kid" senior laughed. "Check it, I'm in the Bx, hit back once you reach the city and I'll tell you how to get to me."

The call ended before Cam got a chance to reply, leaving him only to comply. He jumped back into the car and rushed north.

Tywanna talked nonstop like only people who don't normally have anyone to talk to can. By the time they crossed over into South Carolina he knew almost all there was to know about her. He had to fight the urge not to turn the car around and find this Kathy person and put his foot in her ass.

The girl talked herself to sleep and began snoring lightly. Cam shot a plutonic glance over her thick frame and pretty face and shook his head. The wolves of the world would devour her in the state she was in. He knew he wasn't long for the earth but vowed to teach her everything he could. Teach her to hustle, to survive, the only thing he himself knew.

Tywanna's nap lasted all the way to the New Jersey Turnpike. Amazingly, she picked up the conversation at the exact point she dozed off at. She switched topics fluidly quoting facts and stats along the way. The girl was as sharp as a tack.

Once they crossed the Iconic George Washington Bridge Cam called his father. He repeated the directions to Tywanna as he got them and she mentally wrote them down.

"Turn right," Tywanna recalled as they crossed over the 171st Street Bridge into the Bronx. She navigated them to a basketball court on University Avenue.

"That him?" she asked of the lone man seated on the bench smoking a menthol.

"Think so," Cam replied straining to see the man in the darkened court. He racked a round into his pistol and canceled it in the small of his back. A deep breath later, he opened the door and stepped from the car.

Cameron senior stood up as he watched his son approach. His murderous disposition eased with every step the man took towards him as he came into view.

"Get the fuck outta here!" Senior laughed heartily as his look-a-like son neared. "A-yo B, you look just like me! I was about to wet your ass!"

Cam senior lifted his shirt to reveal the handle of a large automatic to prove his claim.

"Damn we do look alike," Cam acknowledged as he looked the man up and down.

The two killers didn't embrace, shed tears and rock back and forth. Instead, they slapped five and took a seat on the bench. The conversation built slowly but was at full boil as they got to know each other. It was two full hours when Tywanna urgently broke up the revelry.

"I gotta pee!" she announce from the car.

"A-yo, who that?" Senior asked curiously.

"Your granddaughter. Her name is Tywanna too."

Chapter 11

Deidra got up early as was her habit and set off into her tiny kitchen to cook. She almost walked by the stranger sleeping on the sofa. Sleepovers were something that didn't occur in the Forrest household so she rushed into her sons room to investigate.

"Cameron!" she whispered urgently trying to wake her son but not the guest.

"A-yo, chill ma, I'm sleep," senior grumbled and turned his back.

"Cameron Forrest! Who is that man sleeping on the sofa?" She demanded still in a whisper.

"Who? Oh, that's your grandson. Now let me sleep!" he pleaded, and pulled the blanket over his head.

"My what? Grandson!" Deidra exclaimed.

"Ma!" Senior groaned painfully, sending his mother away to investigate on her own.

Grandma Deidra tipped back into the living room and hovered over the sleeping man. He shared their caramel completion as well as course brown hair, but his back was to her preventing her from seeing his face.

That's how Cam found the woman an hour later when he finally awoke. He rolled over to find the pretty elderly lady staring down at him.

"Oh my god! You are my grandson!" she screamed when she finally got a good look at him. "You look just you're your father, and my late husband!"

"Morning ma'am," Cam smiled in his best southern hospitality. "We just came up last night."

"We?"Deidra asked curiously and looked around the room.

On cue, Tywanna emerged from the sacred spare bedroom. The room once belonged to Killa and was maintained just as he'd left it years ago.

"Well hello young lady, and who are you?" Deidra gushed at the pretty girl.

For a reply Tywanna rushed behind Cameron for protection. He was the only one in her life that she trusted, for now anyway.

"This is Tywanna, my daughter," Cam introduced. "Say hey Tywanna."

"Hey," Tywanna said, not offering anymore.

"Oh my, I have a granddaughter too!" she exclaimed and rushed over to hug the girl.

She frowned slightly at the smell coming from the girl as she squeezed her. Tywanna shot a wide eyed glance at Cam who nodded his approval.

"Hey grandma," Tywanna sang now returning the hug and giving grandma a nostril full of underarm funk.

"Let me fix you guys some breakfast! You like cream of wheat?" Deidra offered.

"Who?" Cam and Tywanna asked together. "What's that? Do you have grits?"

"Who?" Deidra asked, "What the heck is a grit? Anyway come on in here and help grandma cook."

Deidra was mildly surprised that the girl was near useless in the kitchen. She had once helped her grandmother cook as a young girl but that was a distant memory now.

Nowadays, all teenage girls were good for one thing- shaking their asses and getting knocked up. She was pleased at how quickly the girl picked up on instructions.Together they whipped up scrambled eggs, biscuits and salmon patties for the two Cameron's.

"After we eat, take a shower, get dressed and you can come with me." Deidra offered as they sat down to eat. She didn't have anywhere specific to go but used the excuse to get the girl to bathe.

Junior and senior scarfed down their meals and resumed their intense conversation.

Tywanna looked around the cramped, yet well stocked bathroom in awe. Grandma was an absolute Diva and had all the hygiene and beauty products to prove it. She reached onto the tub and turned the water on and basked in the warm steam filling the bathroom.

Back in Longs Mississippi the gas had been turned off shortly after her grandparents passed. This would be the first hot bath since then. She peeled off the dingy jeans that she had worn for just under a week. She wasn't immune to her smell, just use to it. Next came the musty shirt and bra followed by soiled panties.

Tywanna giggled from the feel of hot water hitting her body. She lathered up a plush wash cloth with one of the fruity concoctions on the shelf and began to wash. Salon quality shampoo and conditioner degreased her matted, oily hair.

Deidra stuck her head in the door and couldn't believe her eyes.

"Girl you stay under that water until I come back!" She demanded. She reached under the sink and put on the thick yellow rubber gloves she used to clean, and scooped up the girl's crusty clothes. A nose full of female funk changed her mind about washing them, and in the trash they went; the trash compacter down the hall that is.

Deidra rushed over to the dollar store to pick up some clothing for the girl. Ordinarily she would have turned her nose up at the store, this was an emergency. The girl didn't have a stitch of clothes with her. Their sudden appearance and stark baggage set off alarms in the wise woman's head, but she was wise enough to wait to be told. She had already raised two goons, so she knew the signs.

Grandma correctly guessed the sizes and put the cheap bra and panty sets in the cheap basket. Next, a few of the sweat suits the store offered along with socks and cheap sneakers. She would take the girl down 7th Ave when time permitted, but this would have to do for now. Little did she know that it would be six more months before she'd get the girl all to herself.

Tywanna obeyed and was still under the steaming shower when Deidra returned a half hour later. She was so excited about the new clothes she only half dried herself off before putting them on. As she admired the cheap sweat suit, tears began to trickle down her clean face. These were the first new clothes to touch her body in ten years.

Chapter 12

Meanwhile father and son were getting along famously. Cameron senior had an easy solution to his problems with Chris.

"Let me go down there and kill them all," he offered as casually as offering a drink of water.

"Just like that huh?" Cam laughed assuming he wasn't serious. What he had yet to learn is that Cameron Forrest senior was as serious as a heart attack, and just as deadly. He never joked about murder.

"Just like that yo," he replied." Aight, so what about the girl, what are you gonna do with her? I know you ain't taking her on this mission.

"Remember what you told me last night? How you wished you knew about me so you could have raised me? Were you serious or did you just say that shit because it sounded good?"

"Both!" Senior shot back. "It did sound good. Like some shit off a greeting card, but yeah, I meant it."

"Well, take care of her then. Raise her," Cam pleaded. "She can't come with me and she has no other family."

"The way your grandmother took to her I doubt you could get her back anyway."

"Well until then, I plan to teach her everything I know," Cam vowed.

******

"Tywanna, wake up Tywanna," Cam whispered as he shook the girl awake.

"Yes daddy?" She frowned at the interruption of her sleep.

He knew his grandmother might blow a fuse if she figured out what was going on so he waited until the wee hours of the morning to begin her training. Thanks to his father he had all the supplies the curriculum called for. Tonight was marijuana 101.

"Parsley?Oregano? Um...," Tywanna guessed at the mound of greenery her father placed in front of her. "Turnip!No, um collards!"

"No, no, no and no," Cam laughed shaking his head. "This is marijuana. Also known as weed, trees, loud pack, herb, organga just to name a few. It's probably the easiest and safest drug to sell. Sell, not use. Never use drugs you hear me?"

"Yes sir," she nodded urgently to match his tone.

Today's lesson was weighing and bagging. They divided up the one pound package into various dominations. Every lesson was followed by an immediate quiz. The girl passed everyone.

"An ounce, quarter, half," she replied each time he held up a bag, guessing the weight correctly each time.

Next, he'd taught her to weigh by sight and she quickly mastered that as well. The girl picked up instantly, she was a natural. A natural born hustla.

A week after they'd beganshe spoke marijuana fluently, and it was time to move on. It was time she became bilingual.

"Eww! It's bitter!" Tywanna protested and spit the taste from her mouth. "Why you tell me to taste that? My tongue is numb daddy!"

"That's because the coke is top shelf, fish scale," he explained. "Look at it. Remember the taste, the feel, the texture. Only good coke can do that."

To further illustrate, he placed out several batches of blow to teach her how to differentiate bullshit from the good stuff. It took a week before she could spot the best of the bunch no matter what variable Cam would throw in.

Even when he switched different types of cut, she was able to tell by taste what he used. B-12, lactose, baking soda, nothing got by her.

"Now, it's time to teach you how to cook," Cam stated once she mastered weighing by sight.

"Grits?!" She cheered enthusiastically. They both had been missing their down south staple. These damn Yankees had them eating bagels and cream cheese for breakfast.

"No not grits, I wish. It's time for you to learn to cook crack!" He replied.

Tywanna watched curiously as Cam emptied the contents of a baby food jar and rinsed it out. Oddly, she felt some kind of way watching him throw away perfectly good food. She had been able to eat her full meals over the last few weeks, but hunger was something you never forgot. The pain never left you no matter how far you went in life. Some of the most successful people on the planet had shared in the history of deprivation.

"Take an ounce out of that bag and hand it to me," Cam said testing the girl.

"Ain't but an ounce," Tywanna replied, passing it as he fought hard not to smile.

"Put it in the jar with seven grams of baking soda," he directed. "Mix it up and add water."

Tywanna not only followed his directions, she memorized them including the ratios. When her adopted father pulled the surgical mask over his face she did the same.

"I done seen too many niggas fall off and start smoking this shit 'cause they was constantly inhaling the vapors while cooking it up," Cam explained. He was right too.Many king- pins had turned into junkies behind breathing this shit.

Even with the mask on the putrid stench of the crack could be smelled as it bubbled in the jar. Once it was where it needed to be he directed Tywanna to remove it from the heat and cool it with cold water. She placed it on a paper towel to let it dry.

"I'm bugging," Cameron senior announced as the aroma waffled into his nose. The smell roused him from a deep sleep and stood him up.

The man had developed the bad habit of smoking crack laced cigarettes referred to as 'woolies' when he was diagnosed with cancer. He did it mainly to speed up the process as dying slow held no appeal for him. He had been a goon his whole life and wanted to go out in a blaze of glory like all the men he'd sent off into the thereafter.

He quit the second his son and granddaughter arrived. Nothing can subdue a bad habit better than pride, and Cameron senior was a proud man.

"Man I coulda sworn I smelled…" Senior said stopping in mid-sentence as he spotted the crack cookie cooling on the counter.

"Just showing lil' mama how to cook up," Cam explained.

"I did it myself grandpa!" Tywanna cheered holding the rock up for inspection.

"Good Job," He replied before turning to his son. "If you plan on pumping that around here make sure to bring a hammer."

"I already know," Cam replied wearily. He had seen a flash of lust in his father's eye when he first seen the dope but it had disappeared.

"Sell point five twenties and kill all competition," senior advised as he turned to leave. "I'm going back to bed."

"Night grandpa," Tywanna called after him. "Daddy, what's a hammer?"

"You'll see, that's tomorrow's lesson. We 'bout to hit the block," Cam advised.

******

"Like this daddy?" Tywanna asked, as she gingerly sliced through a large piece of crack.

"Not bad," Cam nodded. She was getting the hang of cutting up slabs for retail sales.

Following his father's advice, he'd cut fifty six half grams into twenties. Back home he could have cut them in half again for that same twenty, then again once more, had they been in Mississippi.

The projects like any of the projects had a booming drug trade. Cam watched for a second and determined the flow of traffic coming up from theUniversity through one of the entrance ways.

"This is what we call short stopping," Cam said as he led Tywanna midway through the street and the courtyard. He had effectively cut off all incoming sales from that route. Tywanna was about to get two lessons, short stopping and what it brings.

From their position, they sold the ounce they'd bagged up in a few minutes. A few minutes later a group of teenagers came around the corner.

"And this is what happens when you step on toes," Cam said pulling the hammer he had conceled in the small of his back.

"Told yall!"One of the boys said explaining why their sales abruptly stopped. He brandishedthe small chrome 380 in his hand as they approached.

"Ayo what the fuck?" Their obvious leader barked as they neared.

He was the cute, curly headed boy Tywanna had seen out the window a few times. She heard people calling him Tay which was short for Tayvon. Even now with the snarl on his face and pistol in hand he was still cute. Too bad her daddy was about to murder him. Sucks when that happens.

Her beauty didn't go un-noticed by him either. Cam laughed at the pause he made when he saw Tywanna. It was more than enough time to have killed him if he wanted to.

"My bad shawty, my pops Cameron said it was cool," Cameron offered as he mentally debated which order to kill the kids in.

"Oh shit! That's Mr. Forrest's people!" The one called Pistol Pete exclaimed when he saw the family resemblance.

He was too young to fully grasp why Cam senior was so feared around the hood. It was well established that him or his family was not to be fucked with. What Pete and his generation did know was that the Forrest family produced the killer called Killa. That was more than enough.

"A-yo we got mad respect for yo' peeps, but still fam!" Tay pleaded as he tried to keep his eyes on the man with the gun but the girl had him stuck.

"My bad yo', next time just give me a little spot to pump from. I'll break yall off," Cam offered showing his daughter another aspect of the game.

After that, they leased a bench and sold a few rocks and bags of weed. This wasn't about the money, it too was a lesson.

Cam could tell that all the kids out on the block were working for themselves. There was no structure or order. A real dope boy could move in, organize and make a killing. A real dope boy or girl.

Chapter 13

It wasn't long before grandpa decided to get in on the act.
He too had a lot he could teach the girl. Besides, every woman
needed to learn how to protect herself in this sick society.

Since Cam kept Tywanna out all night he took the morning
sessions. Only problem was, this was when they both slept.

"Grandpa!!!" Tywanna whined as senior roused her from her
sleep.

"Shhh girl, come on!" he demanded in a whisper hoping not
to wake his son. "Get up and get dressed."

Tywanna sluggishly responded and got up out of the bed.
Since hygiene still wasn't too high on her priorities she slid into
the sweat suit from the day before. Her great-grandmother
wanted to take her shopping but had yet to get the girl to herself.
Plus the poor child who was used to nothing was completely
satisfied with the baggy sweats. Cameron senior led her up the
gravel covered roof tops to begin their first lesson.

"Do you know how to fight?" He questioned sternly.

"Yessir!" She replied confidently, "been fighting my whole
life."

"Let's see then," he said and threw a straight jab at her face.

"Hey!" Tywanna yelled as she got popped in the mouth.

"Thought you said you could fight! Why didn't you block it,
or at least duck?" grandpa asked as he shot another straight
right.

"Stop it!" she pouted after getting hit again.

Grandpa didn't stop though.Instead, he kept popping her until she began to block his hits. Finally, she got frustrated enough to fight back.

"That's it," senior cheered as she threw a punch of her own. He blocked the first one but not the second.

"Ohh I'm sorry grandpa!" Tywanna whined as the blow burst his lip.

"Don't be," he said, firing a blow that also burst hers. "Rule one, no mercy. If fighting is the only option, destroy your opponent! Make them submit, no mercy!"

Cameron senior taught the girl everything he knew about boxing. Considering that he was a junior Olympian in his youth, it was plenty, but still not enough. After a month she had a refined hook game and it was time to move on.

"This is Karate Joe," grandpa said introducing a weird little guy in karate pants and slippers.

"Hey," Tywanna sang cordially as the karate man bowed.

The first week was spent on blocks that had Tywanna's forearms so sore she cried. Cried, but didn't quit. Next came strikes, then kicks. A month later she learned submission holds that gave opponent two choices, submit or get your shit broken.

Once those were mastered it was time to learn lethal moves. It was a time to kill. Karate Joe showed her how to snap a person's neck using their own weight and aggression against them.

"Look it grandpa!!!" Tywanna cheered when she made her teacher tap just short of getting his neck broke.

The master was impressed and bowed to her. Next, he taught her the fabled strike that would break a nose spending shards of bone into the brain. That too, earned a giggle once it was mastered.

"She is ready," Karate Joe announced with a bow. He was thoroughly impressed, never had a student learned so much so quickly. The girl was a sponge, and she had soaked up everything he'd taught her.

"We'll see," Senior said returning the bow. He had to put her to the test to see just how ready she really was.

******

"Shit, I forgot my smokes!" Grandpa said as they reached the roof top training facility. "I'll be right back"

"OK grandpa," Tywanna said as she stretched for whatever lessons the day had in store.

He hit the stairway to go back to the apartment just as a known addict named J.J. was going up. They nodded at each other in passing. Senior had often paid the man to carry out small tasks for him. Today was no exception.

"Hey! What you doing up here? This is my spot!" J.J. barked startling the girl as she warmed up.

"Just waiting on my grandpa," Tywanna said looking at the door hoping grandpa would come through it.

"Give me your money!" the junky demanded as he approached.

"I ain't got no money!" She yelled, now angry. She balled up her hands in preparation to give him what she did have. A spare ass whooping.

The junky rushed in and tried to grab her by the neck and caught a flurry of blows that knocked his hat off. He tried again and got the same results. When he reached up to his face and felt the blood and knots left from the blows he got mad.

"OK little bitch," He growled and pulled a knife. "Now I'm 'bout to cut you and rape you"

Now, there are a lot of dangerous things in life. Lion taming, convince store clerk, sky diving, suicide bomber, all dangerous indeed. But, telling a lethally trained, molestation survivor that you're going to rape her, had all of that beat. And then, you call her a bitch!

Every move and technique Karate Joe taught her ran through her mind in an instant as he approached with the knife. When he lunged the first time, she sidestepped the blow and delivered an elbow to the back of his head.

Next, an overhead thrust was reversed and she used his momentum to make him stab himself. He howled so loudly from pain it brought grandpa back up onto the rooftop.

"What the Fuck?" he asked as Tywanna punched and kicked him as if he was a heavy bag in the gym. It was only the crack that kept him standing.

"He….said….he….finna'….rape…me," she said between blows.

When Senior heard the word rape and saw the knife, he sprang into action. Instead of pulling his gun he grabbed the junky by his pants and shirt and took off running over to the edge of the roof and off of the building.

"Come on," he said grabbing Tywanna to get her out of there. As they rushed to the stairwell, she suddenly pulled away.

She ran over and picked up J.J.'s hat and tossed it over the edge.

"Don't forget your hat mista," she smiled watching it float down to where he was splattered below.

"Girl come on!" Senior demanded. She had passed the test with flying colors. Flying junkies too.

******

Next, wouldbe weapon's training. Cam Senior's personal favorite and soon it would be the girls too. It was Hammer time, but before she could actually get her hands on a gun she had to learn everything about them.

"Um... 9mm, 380, 45 ACP," she said naming the different size rounds her grandfather laid out on the table.

"What round does an Ak-47 shoot?"

"Nato 7.62," she shot back quickly.

"A-R 15?"Senior quizzed. "2.23 Or 22 long riffle with conversion."

Cam Senior nodded proudly as she correctly answered every question he'd thrown out, even the trick questions. Next, he trained her in the mechanics of how guns worked. He had her taking them apart and putting them back together while naming each component.

When the time came he drove her over to a gun range in New Jersey. She rambled on incessantly over things her grandfather knew nothing about. Still, he humored her with false enthusiasm.

At the range they rented a variety of weapons ranging from a run of the mil 9 millimeter to an Mp-5 machine pistol. Again academics came first before she got to shoot.

"OK, line the target up using the three dots, just like I showed you. Then squeeze, not pull the trigger," Senior coached from behind.

"Like that grandpa?" Tywanna asked after firing a shot into the forehead of the target.

"Just like that!" He replied proudly. She did the same with each of the guns putting bullets exactly where he told her to shoot.

In a few weeks she was a crack shot able to hit anywhere on a target with any gun. Cam Senior had gotten a kick out of her giggles when he had her spray a three shot burst from a Tech-9 into the target groin. She was turning out to be the son he never had.

Chapter 14

A sudden change in Cam's demeanor had upset the entire Forrest household. It followed a phone call that sent him outside to take a moment of privacy. His spies back in Atlanta confirmed it was time to make his move.

The time to strike at Chris and his crew had come. Not only was he spread thin in a turf that was with both Mexicans and locals, but his pockets were hurting. In a foolish move to hurt his competition he slashed his prices to fifteen grand per kilo. He had taken his business personally which is a recipe for failure in any profession.

His huge ego had goaded him into biting off more than he could chew. He tried to make sure that no one else could eat and it backfired on him.

The dope boy now had to explain his departure to his people one by one. He started with his father. Knowing the killer would understand. He'd understand wanting to kill somebody so badly you can actually taste it.

"When we leaving son?" he asked, including himself. He desperately wanted in on one last gun fight to secure his spot as an urban legend.

What he had planned would make Hip-Hop history. Songs would be written about this one.

"I got this shawty. This is personal, not business," Cam related. He never, ever mixed the two. Especially not after having to kill a baby mama to prove to himself that money and blood didn't mix.

"Besides, I need you to take care of that girl in there," he added.

"Shit, that girl can take care of herself! Trust me on that!" he shot back.

"I'm asking you to do it, please?"

"We'll see," his father said unconvincingly.

******

"Can't you just pay somebody to kill them people?"his grandmother pleaded when Cam came to break the news. "Your father would probably do it on the strength!"

"No grandma, I have to do this myself," he replied. A scowl spread on his face as he recalled the smile on Chris' face when he raised his glass to him. It was the signal to the hit team that killed his wife.

"You and your father will go down there and really, really make a mess, trust me," she urged.

"So, how you and your granddaughter making out?" he asked attempting to switch the subject.

"Oh she's a doll!" Grandma beamed, taking the bait. "I need to get down to Georgia and see the rest of my grandbabies. Tell me again now how you have children by two sisters?"

Cam laughed and explained the Shay and Britney situation. Well, most of it anyway. He left out the part about having her murdered or fucking their mother after the funeral.

They talked and laughed for hours knowing they may not have a chance to ever do it again. With the first two notifications out of the way, it was time to see the girl. This was going to be the hard one.

******

Cam smiled as he stood outside the guest room that had become Tywanna's. He could hear her making karate noises as she practiced her kicks and chops. He knew his father was taking her out teaching her something during the day while he slept.

He wondered why she always gave a slight bow to the strange man called Karate Joe. That would explain it.

"Who?" Tywanna responded to her father's soft knock on the door. She rushed over and pulled it open knowing whoever it was would be welcomed.

"Hey daddy!" she cheered brightly, then adjusted to his demeanor. "What's wrong?"

"Bout that time lil' mama," Cam sighed and plopped down on the bed.

"What time?" Tywanna asked curiously. She shot a glance at the digital clock on the dresser for help.

"Time for me to go back to Atlanta. I want you to stay here with granddad and grandma."

"OK, when are you coming back?" She askedfeeling the finality of the statement.

"Here you go, it's from what we made that night," Cam said skirting the question and handing her a bag of cash. "This is for college, its ten grand."

"I don't want it!" she said, scooting away from the money as if not accepting it would make the problem go away.

"I still have to leave baby."

"Well I'm coming too!" Tywanna said and jumped up to pack.

The girls' desperation was breaking his heart but what could he do? The score was lopsided and had to be settled. Dying he could live with ,but Chris living he couldn't.

This is when she broke into the world famous 'Dope Girl' rant. The sweet, mild mannered girl was so enraged it sent chills up Cam's spine. He was moved but it changed nothing. Murder was murder and some people had to die.

"Easy lil' mama," Cam cooed as he embraced her tightly. The feisty girl swirled and fought to get free but he held on firmly. It wasn't easy though because the push-ups, sit- ups, and pull-ups her grandfather had her doing had paid off. Not only was she pretty, she was pretty strong.

It had taken several minutes until the struggle turned into sobs. Cam held his daughter and let her get it all out. Since men don't cry he remained stoic. When her painful protest subsided he released his hold. After tossing the numbered bank books on the bed he walked out.

Cam walked out to the hallway where he came to find out, men do cry. He plucked one of the tears from his check and stared curiously at it. In it he saw the faces of all the men and women whose lives ended at either his gun or his command. He was feeling real soft until his father came out into the hallway.

******

"I'm not going to college!" Tywanna spat and flung the cash around the room. It was the first time in her life she made it rain cash; it wouldn't be the last.

She seethed in silence for an hour vowing to be a dope girl and everything else her father warned her against. Losing the most important person in her life again was too much. It hardened her heart a little and one day the world would feel the results of it. When she finally ventured out of her room she found her grandmother in pretty much the same state as her.

"Where's grandpa?" Tywanna asked taking a seat next to her distraught grandmother on the sofa.

"Gone. He left with your father, they're both gone," she said with a finality that turned the water works on.

Now it was her turn to be the comforter as she held the old woman in her arms. Hugs always seemed to help the tears flow, so she squeezed until they were exhausted.

Several hours later grandma Deidra's seldom used cell phone began to ring. She immediately took the call, knowing it could only be one of the two people who had the number.

"Hello my son," she smiled upon hearing Senior's voice.

Tywanna smiled along with her eagerly listening to this side of the conversation. She instantly regained her attitude once it was obvious that her father got on the line. She was just waiting for him to ask to speak to her.

"Nope!" Tywanna said stubbornly shaking her head from side to side. "If he wanted to talk to me he shouldn't have left me!"

"Come back to New York and we can talk all you want!" She yelled in the direction of the phone.

"She's not ready to talk yet baby," grandma babied to her grandson. She patted the hostile girl's leg as she spoke in an attempt to comfort them both simultaneously. "Just kill whoever you have to kill and come on back to us."

Chapter 15

If there was a bright side to the men leaving it was Deidra finally having the girl all to herself. It was evident that someone instilled some basic principals into the girl at some point but her lack of proper upbringing was clear. She had a solid foundation built by her grandparents for Deidra to expound.

She had no doubt that her clever grandson was teaching the girl to hustle. Deidra had been in the hood long enough to know what all the empty baby food jars in her kitchen were all about. Somebody had been cooking crack in her pots. The term crackpot came to mind and spread a smile on her face.

Deidra also knew who and what her son was. She knew full well what he was teaching her. She could recall her coming home with black eyes and busted lips initially. Then it was her son coming home with busted lips once she mastered what was being taught.

It was now time for the girl to learn to be a lady. While a boy can manage to become a man without the benefit of having one around, the same does not hold true for a women. It takes a woman to raise a woman.

Many years back a customer of Kathy's sick pedophile service complained because Tywanna had soiled herself. She ascertained that stinking was a way to keep the sick men from touching her. She used her foul smell as molester repellant.

Unfortunately, actions become habit and bathing became a low priority. Back home a couple of cold showers a week would do. Especially, since she didn't have many clothes to change into. Itmade no sense getting clean to put on dirty clothes.

Fortunately, since coming to New York Tywanna began to enjoy hot showers every day. She also learned to appreciate fresh clean clothes to put on even if they'd come from the dollar store.

Her hygiene had greatly improved but grandma still had a lot to teach. It was time for Diva 101.

"Grandma!" Tywanna exclaimed, embarrassed as her grandmother walked in on her shower. Still extremely shy about her nakedness she protested her presence.

"Chill out girl! Grandma needs to show you a thing or two." Deidra said dismissing her protest. "First, here!"

"What's this for grandma?" she asked as she accepted the pink razor. "I ain't got no mustache!"

"No but you got a beard!" grandma laughed at her own joke. "Start with that afro down 'there', then them under arms, legs, everywhere except your head."

Tywanna didn't quite understand but she was obedient. As soon as Deidra cleared the room she cleared the areas. After removing a thick pubic bush she shaved her underarms. Next, came the jungle on her legs and next luckily her grandmother came to check on her.

"No!" Deidra yelled, just as Tywanna raised the razor to her eyebrows.

"You said everywhere but my head," she whined at the admonishment. "Just kidding grandma."

"Well everywhere but there too!" Or else we would have to draw them back on and you'll be walking around looking surprised like the rest of these chicks out here," Grandma chided.

"All that hair makes you sweat and sweat makes you smell," Deidra explained. "Now put your clothes on so we can get you something done to that mop."

Once Tywanna got out of the shower and dried off she immediately felt the benefits of shaving were told. The deodorant glided on easily as opposed to clumps stuck in her underarm hair. She even felt cooler in her panties from shaving down there.

"Gotta buy you some real clothes," grandma said scoffing at the girl's beloved dollar store sweats.

"More sweat pants?" Tywanna asked enthusiastically.

"No real clothes," Deidra replied as their cab pulled to a stop in front of them.

When grandma didn't budge the driver honked the horn in exasperation. He was about to pull off until he glanced over and saw who it was.

"I'm sorry Mrs. Forrest, I didn't know it was you who called," he said, urgently as he rushed to open the back door.

"That's quite alright dear," she replied sliding into the back seat, as he held the door opened and then closed it behind her. She was a true diva, and divas do not open doors. "Take us to Fatimah's on 145th please."

"Yes ma'am, right away ma'am," the diver said eagerly as he pulled from the curb.

"A man will treat you the way you demand to be treated, do you understand?"

"No grandma," Tywanna admitted. She was too green to understand that women got mistreated simply because they allowed it. Excuse one slight, one disrespect and you have given a man the green light to do or say as he pleases.

"You will baby, trust me you will," Grandma relied tenderly.

Fatimah's was an upscale Dominican hair salon in Harlem. They could have called it 'bad bitches only' because that's the only kind of women who frequented the place. You didn't have to be Dominican or Latina, but you had to be fly.

"Ohh, Ms. Deidra! Como esta?" The owner Fatimah gushed when the diva walked in with her granddaughter.

"Bien, Bien, gracias," she replied and launched into a conversation in rapid fluent Spanish. Tywanna was impressed again by the woman. Just yesterday she was chopping it up in Arabic with the man at the butcher shop, proving true divas have brains.

Tywanna watched the pretty women in shock and awe. The way they walked, talked and carried themselves amazed her. She was so enthralled she missed her grandmother's introduction.

"Girl where are you?" Deidra said, reeling her back in. "Say hello to Ms. Fatimah."

"Hey ma'am," she complied in her sweet southern bell manner.

"Oh my god, listen to you! Aren't you the sweetest little thing!" The owner gushed. "Let Ms. Fatimah take care of you personally."

With that, Tywanna was led to the exclusive chair that was coveted by all the women. Some women had to frequent the shop for years before being invited to the throne and having their hair styled by the queen herself.

"Where are you from chica?" Fatimah inquired as she inspected Tywanna's hair. The texture suggested she wasn't just black.

"Mississippi." She replied making it sound like 'Mis sipi' like only a native Mississippian can.

"Ms. Sippi?" Fatimah asked Deidra confused.

"That's Mississippi," Grandma translated with a laugh.

Tywanna had a ball getting her long hair washed and curled. She was giddy as she sat under a dryer reading a fashion magazine like the Diva's did in the movies.

The soft Soca music that served as an audible back drop stirred something deep inside of her. It reached her Latin DNA and caused her feet to tap along with it.

"Wow!" Tywanna gushed at the gorgeous girl staring back at her from the mirror.

"Wow is right little mama. You are all that!" Fatimah cheered.

A scene of dread chased the elation away when she saw some envious glance from some of the other patrons. Even if they did manage to secure the honor of being styled by the queen they wouldn't look like that.

Being cute had often gotten her into trouble back home and it was about to get her into trouble here as well. For some reason, ugly girls hated pretty girls. Tywanna always down-played her looks and did her best to be invisible; It didn't always work.

******

"Uh, uh!Who dat?" Angle, a young hood rat asked as Tywanna and Deidra emerged from their taxi.

Rumors had been swirling around town about the pretty girl staying with the Forrest family, but she was rarely seen. The only ones who saw her were the dealers and users who roamed the night while her and her father trained.

"She must be related to Mrs. Forrest," Zaria replied. "We need to tell Crystalline!"

Crystalline was the leader of the local pack of Ratchet girls. Her Ratchet ass mother named her after a soda she bought as she walked to the hospital to deliver her.

Crystalline was as ugly as one can be, and still be considered human. To make ugly matters even uglier, she embellished the ugly with costumish clothing, wigs and weaves.

Soon a stake out was set up to spot the elusive cute girl. The pack of girls had a park bench that served as their headquarters. They could be found there rain, sleet or snow, Monday through Monday. It didn't take long before their surveillance had paid off.

"Ohh, there she go!" Aqua cheered as Tywanna and her grandmother walked through the court yard.

"She think she cute!" one of them called out, thinking it too.

"Grandma, I think I'ma hafta fight one of'dem gals," Tywanna snarled, as she stared back at the girls starring at her.

"Don't be naïve girl," Grandma replied. "Your gonna have to fight all those girls!"

"Un, uh grandma, just one," Tywanna said. She had been down this road before with Big Bessie back home.

Chapter 16

"Damn it! How did I forget the eggs?" Deidra fussed as she unloaded the groceries. "We can't make macaroni and cheese without eggs."

"I'll run back and get some," Cameisha offered. She was so eager to please her beloved grandmother she would have run to the moon if need be.

"I'll go with you. Let me put my shoes on," grandma said, stopping what she was doing.

"I can go by myself grandma, I'll be alright," Cameisha assured.

"Are you sure?" She asked wearily. She knew the hood rats were on their post looking for trouble. She had seen them jumping on girls from her window for years.

Any girl who wasn't affiliated with someone in their crew was bait. They kept most of the girls in their homes and had all the guys to themselves.

"Well, I gotta go to school soon and you can't come there with me," Tywanna reasoned. She knew she would one day leap this hurdle, and she was ready.

"I will you know!" Grandma laughed. "Be right up in there with my FUBU or ONE UMMAH or whatever y'all kids wear nowadays."

"Y'all? I see I'm rubbin' off on you too," Cameisha laughed. "Now, all I gotta get you to say is 'finna'!"

"I don't think I'll be saying that one! Be careful!"

"I will grandma," she assured as she pulled her laces tight and tied them. Her grandmother smiled when she picked up the newspaper off the table and headed out. She knew what the paper was for; her son had taught her that trick too.

Grandma rushed to the window to watch the show. She wasn't the only one either. Half the project was out enjoying the summer day. When the new girl emerged into the court yard all activity grinded to a halt.

"Hold up yo'!" Tay said, calling an abrupt end to the basketball game.

"There she go! And she alone!" Angle announced eagerly as Cameisha came into view.

This was the moment they had been waiting on. Crystalline swore she was gonna get her if she ever caught her alone. Still, she didn't plan on doing it alone.

"'Bout to check this bitch for trying me!Come on Angle!" she demanded as she jumped up.

Poor Aqua really, really wanted to know how the elusive girl who never said a word or rarely looked in their direction had 'tried' her. Asking questions always seemed to get her in trouble so she stayed mute.

Cameisha smiled to herself as she began discreetly rolling the newspaper tightly behind her back. Not only did her grandfather teach her how to make the disposable club, but he'd taught her how to wield it. These chic's were about to be in serious trouble. It was as hard as a bat and extremely dangerous in the right hands, and it was definitely in the right hands!

"I heard you wa…." Was all Crystalline was able to get out before Cameisha attacked.

The first wack with the club knocked the rest of the false statement on to the sidewalk along with one of her big hamster like front teeth. Cameisha knew there was no way the tramp had heard she said or did anything, so she saw no reason to wait. The girl wanted beef and nowshe had beef. More than she could possibly handle, and minus a tooth.

"Oh shit!" The whole project said as if trained. Like they had an 'oh shit' conductor saying 'one, two, three and …Oh shit!"

The blow was a prelude to a short, but brutal clubbing from the daily news. Angle didn't really want any part of what was going on but had no choice. Not helping a friend who is getting beat up would get you beat up anywhere in the world. In the Bronx it could get you killed. She made a superficial attempt to intervene and paid the price for it.

Cameisha hit Angle from so many angles she thought she was getting jumped. Luckily the make shift club got soft after a while so she got to keep her teeth.

"Y'all get that bitch!" Crystalline demanded to her crew as she attempted to put her tooth back into the hole it had come out of. The rest of the girls jumped up to jump in.

"Ayo, y'all bitches fall back!" Sincerity called out, calling off the attack. "Either fight her head up or sit your ass back down!"

Crystalline and her crew hated Sincerity and they were always 'wished she would' and 'bitch ever try me', but only behind her back. None of them wanted to deal with the project Diva.

Aqua sat down immediately because she was use to taking orders. She was like a puppy trained to sit, bark, and steal and whatever else. Dasia and Zaria looked to Crystalline to tell them what to do.

"I need a one bitch!" Crystalline demanded even though it wasn't really in her heart. What she really wanted was an aspirin and an ice pack, but she had to save face.

She had just gotten her ass whooped and was not eager for another but had no choice. Backing down is worse than getting beat up. Crystalline put her tooth in her pocket and moved in.

"And better not one of you bitches try to jump in," Sincerity barked. "You do and you gonna have to fight me!"

"Me too!" Grandma Deidra who had just came on the scene co-signed.

Cameisha turned her head to see her grandmother with her boots on and Vaseline on her face. The distraction allowed Crystalline to get a punch off. It would be her only one.

Since the club was now useless, Cameisha tossed it aside and threw up them thangs. The real fighters in attendance peeped her technique and grimaced at what was about to happen.

Cameisha was a skilled counter puncher and let her opponent take the lead. Every time Crystalline threw a punch she paid dearly for it. Cameisha would duck or dodge it then unleash a furry.

She punished the girl for every punch, giving her four or five in return. The usually loud project courtyard was eerily quiet except for the thud from the blows that made the ugly girl uglier with each exchange.

Mercifully, Cameisha by-passed many opportunities to kill the girl with any one of the lethal moves she was taught. She also passed plenty of chances to knock the bully out. No, she was going to punish her. Make an example out of her. If anybody wanted it, this is what they had coming.

Pride is one of the most dangerous emotions known to man. It had cost more trouble than it was worth since the beginning of time. How many people had been lured to their death because they had been called out. It may have caused Crystalline her life too if no one stopped the brutal beating. If no one stepped in she may have gotten beaten to death.

"Aight, Aight, that's enough," Sincerity said casually and stepped between the beater and the beatened.

Cameisha was in her zone and quickly squared off at the intrusion. She wasn't sure if she was a friend or foe so she kept her dukes up.

"Trust me little girl, you do not want to see me," Sincerity laughed. "Y'all hoes want to fight her too then line up."

Crystalline's crew all frowned at the ludicrous question. It was like when you were acting up as a child and a parent asked if you want a whooping. Hell no, they didn't want to fight her.

They had just watched the girl who ruled them with an iron fist get her ass handed to her. Of course, they didn't want to fight her. Fuck Naw!

Crystalline was literally bleeding out of every orifice. The beating was so severe it even made her period come on a few days early. She was so relieved to get a reprieve she hugged Sincerity.

"Get your bloody ass off of me," Sincerity said with a shove that sent the girl stumbling. "New girl, go home!"

Cameisha saw no benefit in protesting and did what she was told. She turned to Karate Joe in the crowd of on lookers and traded a bow. She was so happy she skipped home with Deidra in tow.

"Oops, I forgot the eggs," she remembered once they'd gotten home. "It's ok, I'll make rice," grandma laughed.

Chapter 17

"Happy Birthday to you, happy birthday to you," Grandma Deidra sang with the tone of a professional singer as a sleepy Cameisha emerged from her bedroom.

A huge smile spread on her pretty face when she saw her favorite strawberry cake ablaze with 16 candles.

"My birthday ain't until next week!' she exclaimed cheerfully.

"Tywanna maybe, but not Cameisha," Deidra corrected. "Here's your present."

"Oh my god!Oh my god!" Cameisha screamed jumping up and down, as she accepted the gift.

"I take it you like it," grandma beamed proudly.

"I love it! Cameisha Forrest," she said reading her new name on the New York state ID card.

That's one of the perks of New York City, not only can you be anyone you want to be, you can get ID's, birth certificates, shot records and the whole nine yards. The documents could withstand the most scrutinizing eye because they were real. Using connections long established by her son, Deidra secured the girls future by erasing her past.

"Now go get yourself together so you can go up to Yonkers to meet your aunt."

"You're not coming?" Cameisha asked almost sounding scared. She wasn't though, she had been venturing out and around the neighborhood since the beating up of the bully.

It was indeed just like fighting with Big Bessie back home. The whole school teased the smelly child of a crack head until she fought the large girl. It didn't matter that she'd lost every time, it mattered that she'd stood up and fought for herself. If she could go toe to toe with Bessie and live, then they didn't stand a chance.

The first time Crystalline saw her after the beating was a tense moment. It took weeks to recover enough to come outside again, waiting for the lumps and bruises to go away. They did eventually but the tooth was gone for good.

"Ohh, there she go," Zaria said sounding like a tattling child.

"Bitch, leave that girl alone!" Crystalline snapped. "She ain't did shit to you!"

Her rat pack looked at her in disbelief. It was proof that you could beat common sense into a person. Crystalline did not want to go through that again. Who would?

"No baby, I still have some business to take care of. Besides, you need to spend some time with her alone." Deidra explained.

She saw the way the men and boys looked at her when she passed. A time- out was called on the basketball court just so they wouldn't miss her. Grandma also saw how goofy she got when ever that curly head boy was in sight.

Aunt Denise was an alpha female. A boss bitch! She would best be able to train the child on how to deal with the opposite sex. Deidra herself didn't have much experience in that area. She had mated for life and once her husband passed it was over for her. Her life was devoted to her children and travels.

Cameisha and the wolf pack pretended not to see each other as she walked by. It was an uneasy truce that could break at any second. She would be ready when it did.

As the usualfurious game of hoop players grinned to a halt when she walked by, Cameisha had a musical walk without even trying. Her round ass and wide hips would not be still no matter how hard she'd tried.

She and Tay traded their usual smiles when they saw each other. Cameisha still didn't like boys but did like looking at this particular one. There was something about this one.

Still not use to the frigid air conditioning on the bus, Cameisha decided to walk down to the train station. It was only five blocks away to Yankee Stadium and the 4 train, but to the sheltered southern girl it was like time travel.

Those five blocks between High Bridge Projects and Yankee Stadium held more people than the entire town of Longs Mississippi. In those five blocks she saw people of ten different counties and took in their flavors.

She had seen the Jamaicans peddling weed on 165th in a cloud of dense smoke that advertised their product, and the bass heavy, swinging their arms and winding their hips to it.

On the adjacent corner across the street,Authentic pizza was being tossed by one of Mario's sons. The sights, sound and smell were all imported along with the olive oil.

A block over on 164th,Reef was supervising his crew of young hoochies who sashayed back and forth hoping for attention and the trinkets that came with them.

Anyone walking behind Cameisha would have noticed that the extra movement in her sweat pants caused the loud Soca music playing down on 162nd. Beautiful Puerto Ricans communicated in rapid fire Spanish that she couldn't understand, yet it seemed to make sense.

Down on 161st a young Muslim boy was making the call to prayer in Arabic. He held one hand to his ear as he made a beautifully melodic chant that his brothers and sisters in faith instantly responded to. A group of pretty Muslim girls around her age dropped their conversation and headed into the Masjid.

In these five blocks, she inhaled Ganga, sofritto, pasta sauce, and incense. She heard as many dialects as she passed through as many nations.

After paying the token entrance fee, Cameisha climbed the stairs to the elevated number 4 train. The directions her grandmother had given reverberated in her head as she looked at one of the graffiti stained subway maps.

Looking out of the window the Bronx became a collage of colors and colorful people.As she headed uptown when the doors opened at the Woodlawn station, she exited in search of the number 4 bus.

A shivering thirty minutes later she found her Aunts block and pulled the cord exit. She walked two blocks over and took a right just like directed and there was Aunt D.G. beating a man with a stroller.

"Mother fucker are you crazy?" She demanded as she struck him about the head and back.

He didn't answer of course, since he was in the middle of getting his ass kicked. The Diva beat him for as long as he stayed. Finally, he had enough and took off running. She sent him on his way with a kick on his ass.

"Excuse me ma'am. I'm Tyw… Cameisha," Cameisha said introducing herself.

"Oh hey baby!!!" she exclaimed totally switching gears from ferocious to friendly.

"Hey Cameisha giggled as her aunt embraced her tightly. "What was that all about?"

"What baby?" Denise asked sweetly.

"You just whooped that mans ass!!!"

"Oh that!" Dee Gee laughed. My silly ass baby father, he came to take our son to the park and he out there selling drugs! Got crack all in his pampers!"

Cameisha tried and failed not to laugh at the scene. It was hilarious though watching him getting beat with the stroller until it was in pieces. She then passed out his drugs for free to all the junkies on the block.

"Girl that shit ain't funny," Denise said joining in on the laughter. "Besides, this is my block. I run this shit."

Cameisha spent the rest of the day getting schooled on men, business and family. All day Aunt Dee Gee was Queen B, head bitch in charge. Boss bitch, etc, etc.

Nigga's ain't shit, trust no man, can't no man, I can do bad by myself, I wish a nigga would. I don't need no man.

Then her man came home from work.

Now she's all 'how was your day honey?" "Dinner is on the table dear." Rubbing his feet and running his bath. Cameisha being the smart girl that she was, caught the unspoken lesson in that as well.

Chapter 18

Cameisha looked at herself in the mirror and shook her head in disapproval at what she saw. She was still too cute. She had long ago learned her lesson about going to school looking cute; the ugly girls wouldn't have it.

Her first fight with Big Bessie came after her mother in a rare moment of sobriety and sanity decided to do her hair. The cascading curls framing her pretty face was more than the bully who looked like Busta Rhymes in pigtails could take. She beat all the ribbons and bows out of her hair.

No! Being cute was more trouble than it was worth. Subsequently, she pulled her curls into a ponytail and wiped the gloss from her lips.

"That's more like it," Cameisha cheered to herself after "Dumbing" her looks down.

Even with the "plain Jane" and clean face, the girl was pretty. The run of the mill ponytail showed thick waves of long curly hair, good hair.

Likewise, the baggy Capri pants couldn't hide the fact that she had a little ass. The oversized shirt concealed her softball sized breast to her satisfaction. She was all set.

"Going for the Ms. Frumpy look I see," Deidra teased when Cameisha finally emerged from the bathroom.

The quip was despite the fact she was proud that the young girl showed so much modesty. Although she hadn't opened up about her childhood abuse, the signs were there. Cameisha subconsciously cowered whenever a strange man was in the vicinity.

A glance out of the window at the project'sRatchet Girls showed just the opposite. Crystalline and her crew made their way through the project courtyard as loud and as ghetto as possible. None of the girls had on appropriate clothing for school, but the trail of weed smoke they left suggested they weren't going to school to learn.

"You don't like it grandma?" Cameisha whined.

"I love it girl and you," she cooed as she sat a bowl on the table. "I made you some breakfast."

"What's that?" Cameisha frowned at the steaming content of the bowl.

"Grits!" Grandma beamed proudly. "See" Cameisha held her tongue and the lumpy and watery concoction in the bowl. On one hand grandma had tried, but on the other hand she wasn't eating it.

"Um... I, think..." Cameisha stammered in her search for words.

"Girl stop at the deli and grab a bagel then," Deidra huffed, as she took the bowl and dumped it out.

"Thank you grandma," she cheered with a kiss on the cheek. A few words of warning and wisdom later, and Cameisha was out of the door.

Deidra wished she could go with the girl to school. Instead, she settled for watching her from the window as she headed off for her first day of school. Cameisha obviously felt like giving her grandmother a comforting wave but she had already ducked out of sight.

Kids from the High Bridge neighborhood were supposed to attend Taft High School, but a long standing turf war made it too dangerous. Instead, they were sent further uptown to Walton High school on 183rd. This meant the kids had to take the number 13 bus down the hill to Yankee Stadium then catch the number 4 train five stops.

A hush fell over Crystalline and company as Cameisha approached the bus stop. A tense few seconds later, the crew began yapping about some of life's more complex matters.

"You crazy girl, D-Lite's dick gotta be bigger than Young Dap's!" Zaria insisted.

"Why 'causehe taller?" Angle disagreed.

"He is taller! And he got big feet! Crystalline cosigned in favor of their hometown hero.

Meanwhile, Cameisha was engaged in her favorite pastime, math. Mentally she was adding, subtracting and dividing every number she saw. She multiplied the numbers on a license plate by the 166 on the street sign.

As she flipped and bounced numbers around her brain, Tay and his crew of misfits merged from the projects. They all had a slow duck waddle from expensive jeans pulled low off their asses, cascading on top of even more expensive sneakers.

Tay was front and center with a swag so cool it should have had theme music playing. He took a long pull from a thick blunt as he and Cameisha locked eyes. When his gaze grazed her soul she averted her eyes, and went back to her mathematics.

All the girls sang each and every one of their names as they greeted the boys in passing. They nodded and 'what's upped' their replies, as they headed over to Nelson Park. They were going to school too, but not to learn either. The school had a booming weed business that they had a big part in. Half of the three thousand kids in the school smoked pot. It was a gold mine.

There were so many kids, not to mention adults waiting at the bus stop that there was no way they all could fit onto one bus. That didn't mean they wouldn't try. The city ran buses in tandem on that route in the mornings and afternoon.Still, everyone squeezed onto the first bus even though the second trailed closely behind.

Crystalline and her crew were amongst the squeezers and boarded the jammed bus. Aqua was the last one and when no one was looking she flashed Cameisha a smile and discreet wave.

Cameisha cracked a quarter of a smile then prepared to board the second less crowded bus. The bus rumbled down the hill and let them out at the 161st street train station at Yankee Stadium. The school issued bus and train pass granted her access to the next stage of travel. Back home kids boarded a yellow bus to school, here you traveled like grown folks.

Up on the platform all the loud kids gravitated to the back so they could all crowd into the last car. It was as if they had to be in the mix so they wouldn't miss anything. Fuck saying 'I heard', they wanted to say 'I saw' or 'I was there'.

Cameisha along with the rest of the smart, nerdy and un-cool, boarded the train in the middle. The 4 train was on an elevated line so Cameisha stood up the whole way staring out of the window at the city passing by her eyes. How quickly and thoroughly had her world changed.

The herd dismounted the train at 183rd and River Ave and piled out onto the streets. Most went to the school for 1st period while others went to smoke weed and eat.

"Man!" Cameisha whined when she saw that the school didn't serve grits for breakfast either. Instead, she opted for one of the hard donuts everyone called bagels.

Following what she saw the other kids doing she smeared strawberry cream cheese on it and took a bite. When she finished the toasted treat she had forgotten all about her grits.

Walton High School had the same number of people as Longs Mississippi. All those kids milling about in the hallways scared her at first. It reminded her of walking the halls of her small school back home, and boys grabbing her booty.

Things like that didn't happen in the Bronx though. Grab some girls ass here if you want to, just don't be offended when a brother, cousin or father is waiting to murder you when school lets out.

Cameisha took a deep breath and waded into the crowd.Following the numbers over the classes she found her first period class and ventured inside. Since most kids wanted to be fashionably late, she had her pick of any desk. She picked the one closet to the teacher. Aqua took the one next to her.

"Hey, I'm Aqua," she said extending a chubby hand.

Cameisha inspected the hand, the face, and finally, the eyes for traces of treachery, but found none.

"Cameisha," she said politely as she shook the offered hand. "Nice to meet you"

"Where you from?Queens?" Aqua frowned at the trace of accent left in her voice.

Cameisha had practiced night and day to 'tawk' like New York 'tawked', but still, she had a slight twang. If she got upset or angry her speech reverted back to Mississippi.

"Mississippi," Cameisha admitted. She wasn't ashamed. She just didn't want to be different.

"Miss sipi?" Aqua asked.

"Yeah, Miss sipi." She smiled. "Close enough."

"Hola buenos dias. Mi llamo es seniora Campos," a pretty lady sang through a smile as she entered the room.

The students all stared back not understanding a word of what she said. Oddly enough, there were several Puerto Rican and Dominican kids who didn't speak Spanish either.

Cameisha was able to translate the new words simply by the context she used. She understood the cheerful greeting and caught that her name was Mrs. Campos.

The Spanish teacher began with introductory phrases all of which instantly embedded on the smart girls brain. Half way through the class, Tay swaggered in and had taken a seat. His eyes were fire engine red from the weed he'd smoked and reeked of it. Mrs. Campos didn't even acknowledge his presence. She was only there to teach the kids who wanted to be taught. She had no concern for the others.

A lot of kids are only concerned with being cool and they didn't need school for that. 'Cool' was taught by the music and street, then perfected in the jails and morgues.

There were cool funerals held every day in New York.

All of Cameisha's classes went well until she absent mindedly replied "Hure" to roll call in 3rd period.

"Hure? What the fuck is a 'hure'?" A girl laughed from the cool section in the back of the class.

Cameisha turned to see who the antagonist was which only added fuel to the fire. Lola was a trouble maker looking for trouble. And she'd found it.

"Bitch who the fuck you looking at! You don't know me bitch!" she yelled up to the un-cool section where Cameisha sat.

"Call me out my name again and I'm finna' whoop ya' ass," Cameisha advised.

"Finna? Bitch what the fuck is a 'finna'?" Lola laughed using the magic word.

Cameisha had to endure being called the dreadful slander coming up by her mother. It died with her buried in the same card board box. The word now came with a free ass whooping on the house.

"Can't say I ain't warned ya!" she said marching towards the back of the class.

Lola jumped up and met her halfway up the row of desks. She delivered her ass to get whooped and that's exactly what she got. The sound of the 'oohs' and 'ahh's'.

The teacher ran over to break it up but was too late; or Cameisha was too quick because the ass whooping was over by the time she gotten to where they were.

Lola was lumped, leaning and lopsided from the short yet brutal beating. Cameisha had to do a double take to make sure she was the same girl she was beefing with because she now looked so different.

"Um I don't think so," the teacher said as she'd retaken her seat. "To the principal's office young... um lady."

"You to the nurse then the principal," she said helping Lola off the linoleum.

Lola was so disoriented she opened the closet to leave. Luckily one of her friends helped her out. After a quick check up and an ice pack she joined Cameisha in the principal's office.

"Congratulations, you both made history!" The elderly principal quipped sarcastically. "See you girls next week."

Chapter 19

"Girl how in the world did you get suspended on the first day of school?" Deidra asked frustrated.

The woman who had raised the notorious Cameron Forrest senior as well as the infamous Killa was scared she had another menace to society on her hands. She was right, she did.

"I ain't had no choice. She kept calling me out my name," Cameisha pouted.

"You can't fight every time you feel insulted. You gotta pick your your battles," grandma offered.

"She called me a bitch!"

"A what? Well, you were supposed to beat her ass then!" Deidra fumed. She didn't play that either. "Bet she learned her lesson!"

"There go that bitch right there!" Lola yelled pointing Cameisha out to her friends.

'I know this bitch did not just call me a bitch again!" Cameisha thought aloud, as she turned to confront her. She had made up her mind to fight her, and anybody else who disrespected her. Fight every day if need be, there would be no disrespect.

"Reckon I best whoop ya' again," she offered as she approached. Grandma would be upset if she got suspended again but she could live with that. She could not live with the slander.

"Bitch you ain't did shit!" Lola laughed. She wasn't lying because she really didn't recall the beating. She saw the results in the mirror but wasn't mentally present when she received them.

"Beat the tar out ya," Cameisha laughed, sounding every bit like Tywanna.

"Ayo, y'all wait 'til after school so no one gets in trouble," Lola right hand Tovia suggested.

"Sounds like a plan!" Cameisha shot back. She was still too green to understand that the plan was to jump her.

"Bet bitch, after school! Over on 183rd Lola chided. Cameisha fought the urge to attack and turned on her heels. She had no idea that all the girls from the Bronx River projects all stuck together. She had just made a play date with all twenty of them.

******

"Yo what's good mama?" Tay drawled as he plopped down beside Cameisha in Spanish class.

Cameisha frowned as she contemplated an answer. First what was good? And why mama?

"Fine," she replied with half a smile, figuring that reply should cover it.

"Yeah you are," he laughed feeling her up visually.

"Cameisha, que es un problemo?" Mrs. Campos inquired.

"No problemo senorita," she replied in flawless Spanish that impressed them both.

As hard as it was she ignored the cute boy beside her and focused her attention to the lesson. By the end of the class her vocabulary had increased tremendously. She absorbed everything she was given; not just in Spanish but in every class she entered. She was smarter when she left. She even ignored the cat calls and slander from Lola and company during third period history. She figured she may as well let her have her fun considering the beating she had coming.

Word about the rumble quietly and quickly spread through the school. The Bronx River Wolf Pack was especially vicious and had a reputation of stripping girls naked after jumping on them. This of course brought the boys out to see some titties.

"Sup now bitch!" Lola demanded. She was real confident, now that the odds were Twenty to one.

"I was hoping you would say that." Cameisha smiled and moved in. Just as she reached Lola to throw a blow, the wolf pack pounced.

Cameisha knew she was about to get jumped so she focused on Lola. Whatever happened she was getting her ass kicked.

The street exploded in violence as blows were thrown in every direction. Miraculously, Cameisha didn't feel a thing. Luckily, Lola was so quickly defeated it afforded her a chance to glance around. The first thing she saw was Aqua who had knocked Tovia out cold.

"Y'all bitches can't fuck with High Ridge!" Crystalline shouted as she pummeled another girl.

Zaria, Angle and a few more girls from the projects were giving the Bronx River chicks all they could handle.

A police cruiser whipped up to a stop in front of the combatants and watched the fight. After all, who doesn't love a good girl fight? And this was a good one. It wasn't until the glint of a knife caught the officer's eye that they'd broken it up.

"Aight, Aight, that's plenty!" The driver of the patrol car announced through the P.A. system. A quick blast of the siren broke up the fight and dispersed the crowd.

"Hell yeah! We beat them hoes ass!"Crystalline cheered and raised her hand.

"Damn skraight!" Cameisha laughed giving her a high five.

The Rowdy project chicks rambled over to the train for the ride home. The combatants were now on opposite sides of the platform hurling insults at each other,

"Y'all hoes ain't did shit!" Tovia yelled from across the divide. It was obvious she was their leader or their spokesman.

"Shit we can go again!" Crystalline shouted back since she was theirs.

The argument escalated to the point of throwing bottles and debris from the over flowing trash cans. Luckily, both trains came and took both sets of girls in separate directions.

"Ayo, you with us now!" Crystalline announced to Cameisha and everyone listening. Everyone paused waiting for her to reply. A slow smile spread on her face as she accepted being accepted.

Even though she was officially a part of the crew Cameisha stuck to her routine. She only spoke when spoken to and didn't hang out with the girls except for at school.

She and Aqua did manage to become friendly, if not friends. Cameisha grew extremely fond of the large girl with the slow wit and quick smile. Soon they were friends and very protective of each other. No one could tease either one in the presence of the other.

The beef between the Bronx River girls and the High Bridge hood rats simmered all year. There were a few flare ups and squirmishes but the school security managed to contain it. Police posted up each day after school to prevent them from killing each other.

Of course the bee went viral with death threats speeding across the globe via internet. Even girls in war turned Bosnia were shaking their heads. Once school was out there was nothing more the school could do. If the two groups bumped heads anywhere over the summer it was on. Somebody was gonna get killed!

Chapter 20

"Ayo Meisha! What's up?" Zaria called out as Cameisha and her grandmother returned home through the court yard. "Come kick it with us."

Cameisha tried to shoot a quick head nod for reply so Deidra wouldn't catch it.

"Um Meisha, your friends are calling you," she said knowingly.

"I don't hang out with them grandma, I swear!" Cameisha said embarrassed.

"It's ok baby. I know you need people your own age to talk to. And no matter what, stay true to you. Never be a follower," Deidra warned.

She knew the girl had to develop her social skills to be well rounded in life. Unfortunately, the projects didn't have much more to offer then Crystalline and company.

"Once we put the groceries away go spend a few minutes with the ...uh...girls," Grandma said getting stuck on the word. She was too old to say hoes like she really wanted to.

"Ok grandma," Cameisha agreed as usual. She really had no interest in sitting on the park bench dong nothing ,but she could handle a few minutes.

Cameisha still enjoyed spending her free time learning. She was now fluent in Spanish and chatted with her South American internet friends flawlessly. If she could master that, surely she could stand to 'kick it' for a few minutes.

As soon as she learned 'how' to 'kick it'.She googled it. According to her research, there really wasn't much to it. She wouldn't need any special clothes or gear, just 'kick it'.

"Sup Meisha," Crystalline asked scooting over so Cameisha could sit by her side.

"Chilin yo," she replied quite authentically as she took the seat.

Cameisha was tickled to death to hear her new nickname Meisha. All the cool kids had either a nickname, or a 'they call me', or just an initial. She was now a cool kid.

"Bout time you come hang out with us. We been thumping with them Bronx River mutts all year with yo' ass!" Zaria stated.

"Them hoes ratchet to death yo'! All them bitches do is sit on the bench in they projects all day!"Angle announced ironically.

Cameisha bit her tongue at the statement and just nodded instead. For the next hour she nodded, giggled and 'that's what's up', to the ghetto girls banter. A lot of what was said was foreign but still she soaked it up.

"There go your moms and Mi-Mi," Angle said tapping Zaria to alert them to their presence.

"Zaria, I have things to do this evening you need to come here and take care of your child," her slightly older mother announced.

Chill ma, why you sweating me dang!" Zaria huffed at the interruption. Her mother had plans to 'kick it' too and wasn't bringing her grandchild.

"Aight yo', I'll be up in a second," she relented.

"You have a baby?" Cameisha asked in shock and awe.

"Yeah man, me and Jo-Jo," Zaria sighed. She didn't spend much time with her child either, but at least she was happy about him.

"Me too," Crystalline and Dasia said at the same time.

"How bout you?" She asked turning to Aqua.

"Naw, my mother had me fixed," she said sadly. "I can't have no babies."

"Sup y'all? Y'all smoking?" Tay asked the crew through Cameisha.

Cameisha basked in his hazel eyes for a second before turning away. He was nice to look at but that's all; she still didn't like boys. He was cute though.

"Y'all bitches pony up so we can blaze," Crystalline demanded sending the girls onto their pockets.

"I'll let y'all get this ….ounce for the fifty, since I fucks with y'all," Tay smiled, holding up a sandwich bag of brownish weed.

"That's not an ounce," Cameisha blurted out before she could stop herself.

"Huh?" Tay asked confused.

"You said an ounce, that's not an ounce," she said plainly since the cat was out of the bag.

"It's not?" Tay said now pretending to be surprised.

"Nope, about a half," she replied exactly.

"Aight, I'll let yall have it for the quarter then," he relented. "Since I fucks with y'all."

"Here you go," Crystalline said handing over the collection and accepting the weed.

"My ass broke yo'. We need to go boosting so a bitch can get her paper straight," Zaria announced. Cameisha made a mental note to Google 'Boosting' as soon as she got in.

"For real though," Crystalline agreed. "Yall bitches be ready tomorrow.We going down town."

"Well, I gotta go upstairs now. My grandmother be buggin' yo," Cameisha announced in flawless ebonics.

"Stay and blaze one!" Angle pleaded.

"I can't. I'll see y'all tomorrow," she said begging off, and unwittingly agreeing to go boosting.

******

Cameisha forgot to Google 'boosting' and had no idea what she was getting herself into. She met up with her new crew and prepared to go downtown. Since the school issued bus passes were worthless during the summer they set out on foot to Yankee Stadium.

As usual, Cameisha kept quiet and soaked up her surroundings. Crystalline was aggressive, loud and mean but it was just a front. Deep down, she was lonely, insecure and shy. She felt that dominating people was far better than being dominated.

Zaria had the looks of a young super model or video vixen depending on who got to her first. She was smart as well; smart enough to dumb down her looks to appease Crystalline.

Dasia was a bit of a plain Jane, the type dudes marry. Smart, but a follower who played her position. Again, the type dudes marry. She had an interesting quirk of coughing as she laughed. She had unnecessarily gotten the Heimlich maneuver several times growing up. Her ass was gonna be in trouble if she ever started choking for real.

Angle was as ratchet as her ratchet ass mother. She was destined to make babies and dwell in these same projects for the rest of her life. Might end up in a Queen Pen story.

Aqua was, well Aqua. She was a big pretty girl, who was a little slow. Thick and pretty like young Queen Latifa.She was taken advantage of by most men who came into contact with her. Her mother had her tubes tied at 13 because her husband kept getting her pregnant. Now she only fucked when and who Crystalline allowed.

Aqua was loyal and extremely protective, especially towards Cameisha who always heard her out no matter how insane the subject.

Cameisha noticed her companions clothing and wondered if she had rubbed off on them. Instead of the usual too tight or too short, they all wore loose fitting clothes. She still didn't like her clothes fitting too snug because it drew attention to her body. Plus she needed a little room to move in case she had to kick somebody in the mouth.

The case wasn't the same for the girls, they were dressed to steal. Their loose clothes would allow them to put on several layers of stolen merchandise underneath. They also carried large collapsible tote bags for even more loot. Finally, each girl carried an old fashioned can opener. These were used to remove the security devices the department store attached to the clothes.

Each girl was also armed with a list of specific items to boost for their paying customers. They could get one third to one half of the ticket price. Of course, they were going to steal a few items for their own children as well. Why do you think all the project babies stayed fly? If the poor residents couldn't afford regular housing, they certainly couldn't afford buying Jordan's every couple of months for rapidly growing toddlers.

The girls made it to the train station and lurked near the token booth. Cameisha wondered why no one got in line and bought any tokens, she soon got her answer when they heard a train approaching.

"Now!" Crystalline yelled and took off running. She hopped the turnstile like an Olympic hurdler with her girl's right behind her.

Cameisha didn't want to be the odd man out or get left behind so she followed as well. The clerk in the booth screamed as if the five fares would be deducted from her pay check or she would lose her job. Neither, was the case, she was just petty.

"Hell yeah, hell yeah!" Zaria cheered giving everyone high fives as the doors closed with them all safely inside.

Nine times out of ten you could catch a free ride in this manner, timing was everything. On that tenth time transit cops would be waiting on the platform when you got there. Once, some dunce who had just robbed a bank got caught hopping the turnstile. He had over a hundred grand on him but old habits die hard.

Cameisha laughed along with her friends as they cracked jokes on everyone on the train. It wasn't really funny but it was fun and exciting coming from Longs Mississippi. A long, loud boisterous ride later, the pack of girls emerged onto 34th street and all the smiles and banter came to an abrupt end. It was now time to get down to business.

The girls fanned out in different directions and went to work. Cameisha followed Aqua as she hit the men's clothing. She removed the security devices Cameisha thought was possible, and concealed them under her clothes. Next, expensive shirts disappeared with the jeans.

Satisfied with the haul, Aqua turned on her heels and walked briskly towards the exit. Zaria too had completed her task and walked out ahead of them. The girls didn't speak, or so much as look at each other. Once you were loaded down you were on your own. They would kick it once they get back to the block.

"I struck real good! I'm getting some pizza and wings and cake! I love cake," Aqua cheered once they were safely on the D train heading back uptown. It was clear she planned on eating her proceeds.

"Ohh, I got my son fly ass jeans! He gone be the flyest boy in daycare," Zaria announced showing what was important to her as well.

Once they got back to the projects Aqua made a beeline to where the boys where hustling. When she started pulling the designer clothes out they scrambled to grab what they could.

"Let me get them ONE UMMAH jeans and that shirt," Tay ordered. He locked eyes with Cameisha as he pulled out a sizable roll of drug money.

This time she didn't look away. Aqua collected almost five hundred dollars from her haul. She gave fifty of it back for a half ounce of weed that Cameisha vouched for.

"Tay likes you!" Aqua sang as they left the trap.

"Oh," Cameisha replied as if she didn't know. In fact she liked him too she just didn't know what to do about it.

Chapter 21

Heavy rain pushed the girls from their park bench perch to indoors. Angles house was the official headquarters for situations like this. Her mother Nita didn't mind them smoking weed as long as she could get a pull or two.

The mood was festive from all the weed smoke in the air. Even Cameisha was giddy from inhaling second hand Kush. The munchies set in calling for pizza, hot wings, and of course, cake for Aqua.

Cameisha still wouldn't take an active role in boosting but contributed money from the stash she and her father hustled up. It was her college fund but one could argue that buying weed was higher learning. Actually, she was learning social skills. Learning to follow so she could one day become a leader.

"Oh, this my shit right here!" Angle yelled as the latest D-Lite banger came on the radio. She jumped up and began gyrating to the music.

"Hey!" Nita sang and joined her daughter dancing. One by one they got up and danced to the hit song. Yep, even Cameisha.

"What kinda dance is that?" Dasia asked amused at Cameisha's movements. Of course, the only dance moves she knew was the 'fat-fat' dance but she certainly wasn't going to admit it.

"It's called...the ...um, Mississippi. It's what we do back home," she replied using her original accent as proof.

"Let me see," Crystalline said coming next to her. She then mimicked Camesiha's every move. The rest of the crew was next. Soon they were all doing the 'fat-fat' but just didn't know it.

"Girl you need to come to Brandford Place with us tomorrow!" Zaria proclaimed.

"For real though. Brandford place is the shit!" Nita co-signed.

"Ma! You can't be coming up in the same parties I be in!" Angle groaned. Her ratchet ass mother had no problem with hanging out with teenagers. They were after all, her peers mentally.

"What's Brandford place?" Cameisha asked intrigued.

"It's the shit!" Nita repeated.

Brandford place was more of a where than a what. It was actually a dead end street off of Burnside Ave a little further uptown. The last building on the block had an empty apartment that had been commandeered for use as a teen club.

Since kids couldn't get into any of the grown up clubs so they'd made their own. Kids from all over the Bronx flocked to the spot each Saturday night. Five bucks got you in and it was B.Y.O.B., which in the Bx meant to bring your own blunts, burners and bandages.

It may have been all the glowing endorsements, or the contact high, but something made the recluse agree. She even surprised herself when she said 'okay'.

"Girl, you ain't going nowhere with us dressed like that!" Zaria exclaimed. The tone was friendly but she was serious.

"For real though. Just come by my crib and I'll give you something to wear," Dasia offered.

"You know we gotta represent!" Crystalline cheered. She was right too because it wasn't enough for you to be a fly individually, your whole crew had to be right.

******

"Are you sure about this?" Grandma Deidra asked over dinner. She had already given her permission for Cameisha to attend the party, but was now she having second thoughts.

"I guess," she replied, having doubts of her own now. It seemed like a good idea yesterday when she was caught up in the moment, but now, eh.

"Well, I know I don't have to warn you about boys, and drugs and being careful," Deidra said warning her about boys and drugs and being careful.

"No grandma," Cameisha laughed at the slick admonishment.

After a shower, Meisha pulled her hair into a ponytail and pulled on her sweats. She was cool with how she looked but still headed over to Dasia's apartment to get dressed.

"No! Way!" Cameisha protested looking at herself in the skin tight jeans Dasia offered. They were just as tight as the ones she had on.

"Girl you look good! And you got a fat ass, no homo," Dasia complemented.

"Un uh, feels like I'ma get a yeast infection messing with these tight britches!"

"OK, first of all, these are pants not… britches," Dasia laughed.

"Whatever they are I ain't wearing them!" Cameisha huffed as she peeled them back off. "What else you got?"

The girls spent the next hour picking and rejecting items from Dasia's extensive boosted wardrobe. Finally, they settled on capri pants and a designer tee.

"Now this hair," Dasia exclaimed moving on her ponytail.

"Is staying just like it is!" Cameisha insisted. She still didn't want to draw too much attention to herself.

The girls headed over to Angles apartment for the rest of the pre-party preparations. That meant smoking weed and drinking wine coolers.

"Un, uh girl you gotta smoke with us tonight!" Crystalline insisted when Meisha passed on the blunt.

"For real yo! You fucking up the rotation," Zaria laughed.

"I ain't never done it before," Cameisha whined eagerly.

"OK, I'ma blow ya'a gun," Aqua offered when the blunt had made its way to her.

"What I gotta do?" She asked as Aqua put the lit end of the cigar in her mouth and began blowing a steady stream of smoke.

"Breath!" All the girls yelled causing Meisha to rush to comply. She leaned in and inhaled filling her virgin lungs.

"That's it, now hold it," Nita instructed just as she had taught her own daughter to smoke weed.

Cameisha obeyed and held the hot smoke for as long as it would stay down. Finally, it forced its way out in a coughing spell. When the hacking cough subsided she was all smiles.

"I feel it!" she giggled as the warming glow of the THC spread through her person.

"Damn right you do! This that Dro!" Crystalline bragged.

"It's not Hydro Phonics. Actually it's a nice mid grade of regular. Tennessee or Kentucky," Cameisha blurted. Everyone just looked at her as if she spoke the phrase in Korean.

"Um…anyway, let's bounce,"Crystalline ordered. They all fell in line behind her and exited the apartment. A crowded cab delivered them to the train station.

Now too cute to hop the turnstile, they all purchased tokens. Cameisha watched the darkened slums pass by underneath as the train rumbled uptown. Once they reached Davidson they got off and hoofed it over to Branford Place.

The thunderous bass line of an Erv-G song seemed to vibrate the entire tenement building as they ascended the stairs. Aqua paid the admission to the man at the door holding a Tech nine machine gun like it was legal.

Cameisha admired the hardware even though she preferred the H&K Mp-5 herself. He was the only security to speak of but not the only one with a gun. In fact, most of the packs of boys from different projects and hoods had at least one shooter among them. This was the Bx you know.

The girls entered the dim, smoke filled room and blinked it into focus. The first thing Cameisha saw was Tay gripping a microphone ferociously spitting violent lyrics that the crowd devoured. He acknowledged her with a head nod and went about his rhymes.

"Come on y'all, let's turn this shit out!" Crystalline ordered marching to the center of the dance floor. When she broke out doing the 'fat-fat' dance her girls followed suit.

They, of course added their own flare to it and made it their own. All the other girls watched in envy, mad that they didn't get the scoop on the newest dance. This was only the epi-center, all in attendance would take it back to their hoods and it would spread like wild fire.

"What's that called?" A girl worked up enough nerve to ask.

"The Mississippi," Zaria said breathlessly as she worked it. The girl stood next to her and did what she did until she had it down.

"Hate them bitches," Tovia grumbled at the attention the High Bridge girls were getting. Lola couldn't help but cringe upon hearing the 'B' word used. She had gotten her ass whooped so thoroughly because of it she hadn't used it since.

"Me too," Lola said even as she mimicked their dance moves.

"Let's step to those bitches!" Tovia demanded and led the way. She pushed onto the dance floor bumping girls out the way.

"Fuck is your problem?" Zaria spat, ready to thump. Her girls saw what happened and rushed to her side. The two groups squared off and began yelling at each other. This was to get their blood pumping and ready for battle.

Before they got a chance to set it off, the apartment erupted in violence. Dudes from Sound View Projects had a long standing beef with dudes from Co-op City. Now that they were in the same place it was going down.

That's black folk for you, a comma is enough to divide them and once divided they have no problem killing each other. The particular feud began long before any of them were born. These kids had no idea what they were dying over, but die they did.

'Brrrrrrrt', a semi- automatic something belched spraying the room with bullets. Kids scrambled to get out anyway they could. That meant squeezing through the front door and climbing out the fire escapes.

It's an unwritten rule that when a party gets shot up you head home. There's no time to re-group or take a head count, go home! Luckily the journey was imprinted on Cameisha's brain so she rushed towards the train station.

"Ayo Meisha! Come on!" Tay called holding the door of a gypsy cab open. The Spanish driver yelled rapid curses at him to close it so he could pull off.

It only took a split second to weigh the options of train versus cab before she joined him in the back seat. She calmed the driver in flawless Spanish and gave him their destination.

"You Puerto rican?" Tay asked, assuming all Spanish speakers were.

"No," Cameisha replied stopping just short of saying Mexican. "I took Spanish last year."

"Aight, Aight so what's up ma? You got a man?" he said dropping his voice a few octaves to sound like one.

"No," she giggled shyly.

"Well you do now. You my girl from now on," Tay said firmly, nodding his head since he agreed with himself.

"Um, ok," she nodded. "What I gotta do?"

"A lot," he replied seductively then switched gears."We gonnago on a date tomorrow so dress fly."

"OK," then came the reply again causing Tay to think about asking for more.

Once they arrived at the projects, Tay paid the driver and they got out. An awkward moment that could have led to a first kiss was quickly ruined by her friends.

"Ayo, Meishawhere Crystalline?" Dasia asked, in her usual theatrics. She had a way of making any and everything sound major. Everything with her was 'yo!!', 'oh shit!!!', or 'check it!' Drama queen with a capital D.Q.!

"Tomorrow," Tay ordered and slipped away into the darkness.

"I just got back, where everybody else?"Cameisha replied scanning the projects. Just then Aqua and Zaria appeared in the court yard.

"Where Angle and Crystalline?" Zaria demanded. "We took the train and ain't seen 'em".

Chapter 22

"Hmpf!" grandma pouted as Cameisha entered the living room. She was heated about this so-called date she had agreed to.

"Grandma..." Cameisha whined with a chuckle. "If you don't want me to go I won't go."

"No, no go ahead, have fun," Deidra acquiesced. It wasn't so much the date she was concerned with it was 'the who'. She knew the cute curly head boy sold drugs. Ninety percent of the males from these projects sold drugs at one point or another. It was like a right of passage. TheGhetto Barmitzvah. No, her main problem was all the curly headed little babies running around the projects.

"I spoke with Auntie D.G. last night," Cameisha offered knowing that would soothe her nerves.

"Ayo Meisha!" Tay called up from the courtyard.

"Bye grandma, I'll see you in a couple of hours," she cheered ready to hit the door.

"Chile, I wish you would let some nigga holla' for you! Or honk a horn or tell you to meet him!" Deidra barked.

"Boy, if you plan on taking my granddaughter anywhere you better come up here and get her and bring her back right here! untouched!" She yelled down to him.

Cameisha started to protest but grandma had her 'no protest' look on her face so she sat down. A minute later Tay tapped on the heavy project door.

"Yes, may I help you?" Deidra asked as she pulled it open.

"I'm supposed to be taking Cameisha to the movies," Tay smiled in an attempt to charm the lady.

"Hmpf, what time will you be returning her home? Right here, to this apartment where you get her from?"

"The movie starts at two, so around five?" Tay replied. He needed to get back early himself so he could hit the trap. It was the first of the month and government money was in abundance.

"Forty thirty," grandma demanded just to be difficult.

"Grandma!"Cameisha groaned in embarrassment.

"Don't grandma me! And definitely don't great-grandma me! You feel me?"

"Bye grandma," she laughed shaking her head as she left.

Tay walked her the long way through the projects before heading over to Ogden Ave to catch a taxi. This was done to show off the fact that he had bagged the exclusive new girl. Even though Cameisha had lived there over a year, her rare appearances still classified her as new.

Cameisha had hoped they were going downtown to the iconic Times Square to catch a movie, but when Tay led her to the D train instead of the one heading downtown, that meant Fordham Rd. Tay was a hood dude and preferred the ghetto shopping district to the tourist trap.

"You hungry?" He asked detouring into a pizza shop.

"A little,"she replied even though she was starved. Aunt D.G told her that if a man wanted your time he had to feed you so she skipped lunch.

Cameisha mimicked what Tay did and shook a pile of parmesan cheese and red pepper on her greasy slice of pizza.

They both folded them lengthwise and let the excess oil runs off the paper plate. Combined it was enough grease to fry a chicken. Iced tea that tasted nothing like ice tea washed down the pizza and they were off again.

"Ayo check this ma!" Tay exclaimed at the sight of a gaudy piece of jewelry in one of the slum jewelry stores that dotted Fordham Rd.

Cameisha followed him inside as he admired the large medallion crusted in cheap diamond flakes. The Jewish jeweler was skilled enough to set the chips in white gold that made them flash like superior grade stones when the light hit them.

"Five stacks yo, I'ma cop this by the end of summer. That's my word." Tay swore.

"It's nice," she lied to appease him. At that point the idea of extravagant jewelry was silly to her. She had done enough research to know that diamonds were neither rare nor expensive.

"Nice? This shit is dope!" Tay corrected. He paid homage to the piece for a few more minutes before tearing himself away.

"OK, we got ANIMAL or TRAP HOUSE," Tay said skipping the middle movie listed on the marquee.

"I wanna see THE PREACHERS WIFE," Cameisha insisted. She would have been content with the other two but Aunt D.G. told her that if a dude is really feeling you he'll sit through a chic- flick with you.

"That's what's up," he agreed and approached the ticket booth. Cameisha pumped her fist 'yesss!' as she followed.

Aunt D.G said that if a man was feeling you he would buy you whatever you asked for from the concession without comment or complaint. She tried him up and pointed at stuff she had no intentions of eating. He bought it all without a word. He was feeling her.

Cameisha was so distraught and disgusted by the drug induced antics of the Preacher's Wife she got up and walked out. It was an award winning adaptation of the bestselling book but it hit too close to home. Watching a woman subject her children to abuse to soothe her craving was too much. It was her life.

"What's wrong yo?" Tay asked as he caught up to her outside.

"I hate that bitch!" Cameisha fumed.

"Yeah she was that bullshit," Tay agreed assuming she meant the character on the screen. In truth she meant the character from her own life.

This was the first time she thought of her mother in a long time. She didn't ever try to stop the tears from falling once they began. Aunt D.G. said a good cry was like a douche for your soul;whatever that meant.

"You aight?" Tay asked slipping a comforting arm around her shoulders. She leaned into him and let it all out.

By the time they reached the Grand Concourse, Cameisha's soul was spring time fresh and she felt better. He stuck out his hand causing a taxi to cross all lanes of traffic and stop in front of them. Hand in hand, in silence, they rode back over to High Bridge. Tay planned to get a kiss this time and she planned to let him, but...

"Ayo Meisha come on!" Aqua yelled as the couple emerged from the cab.

"Crystalline got shot last night! We heading to the hospital now," Dasia added.

"Go head yo'. I'll catch up with you later," Tay sighed. He rushed off into the drug traffic before she could respond.

The crew of girls squeezed into another taxi and raced to the hospital to check on their leader.

"I thought she was with you?" Zaria demanded to Angle.

"Un,uh, when them niggas started bussin' we just bounced. I got in the cab with some dude and stayed over his house," she shot back defensively.

"What dude?" Dasia asked excitedly, "You fuck him?"

"I don't know his name, and of course I fucked him. He paid for the cab and smoked a blunt with me!"

Cameisha frowned at the prospect of having sex with a dude you didn't even know. Aunt D.G. said the coochie was a commodity and you get its worth. Hers was priceless.

"Crystalline Johnson!" Zaria demanded as they stormed the information desk.

"She's in 701, medical ICU," the nurse replied grimly. The girls had no idea of what ICU stood for and thus no idea how bad off their friend was.

"701." Zaria relayed even though her crew was close enough to hear for themselves. She turned away and marched towards the elevator as the nurse called behind them.

"Hey! You girls can't go up there!" She yelled to their departing backs, "security!"

The crew didn't ignore the warning they were too concerned about their friend to hear it. They rushed into the first available elevator and raced up to the 7th floor.

"In here!" Dasia called out when she read the room number over the door. They followed her into the room and stopped dead in their tracks.

"The fuck!" Zaria spat at the sight of Crystalline.

"Fuck wrong with yall?" Crystalline asked with a week laugh.

"You aight yo?" Aqua asked.

"Hell no! I got shot!" she croaked, "high as a mother fucker from whatever they got my ass on!"

"Where you got hit?" Dasia asked as they finally approached her bedside.

"In the back yo'. Yall bitches left me!" She frowned.

"Left you!? Girl yo' ass was the first one to dip! You hit that fire escape like yo' ass was on fire!" Angle laughed.

"Speaking of hot asses, I seen you dip in a cab with some nigga."

"She fucked him too!" Aqua reported.

"I was right behind you 'til my shit just went numb. I ain't even feel the shit yo'.My legs just stopped working," Crystalline relayed. The fact that she had been hit in her spine and would never walk again wasn't passed along yet.

The hospital staff wanted to inform a parent or guardian before giving the grim news to the patient. Of course, they would have to wait until her mother got in from her own night on the town. She too went home and fucked a dude without getting a name. He did smoke a blunt with her though so it was all good.

"You guys can't be in here!" the security guard said sternly from the doorway.

"Your friend needs some rest so the medication can work and she can go home," a young handsome black doctor added. His pretty presence prevented the outburst that was sure to follow the guard's statement.

"Okay," they all sang flirtatiously together.

"Y'all fall back. I'll be home in a day or two," Crystalline ordered. She stopped short of saying as soon as I can feel my legs again.

******

"What now!" Zaria griped when they returned to their projects. It looked like the whole 44th precinct was milling about.

"Look it, oh shit!" Dasia said pointing towards the parking lot. The police had a group of men and boys attached to one long chain. They were being led into the back of a waiting paddy wagon.

Tay was at the end of the chain. He made eye contact with Cameisha and shook his head. He and the rest of the dealers got caught red handed with dope, their summer was over.

Chapter 23

Cameisha still had almost all of the ten grand her father had left her when he left. Add that to her grandmother supplying all her needs and breaking her off lovely, and even she couldn't explain why she was clad in baggy clothes heading downtown to boost. She often accompanied her girls on the mission that kept them in weed and weave but never participated, until now that is.

Since Crystalline was still in the hospital Angle assumed the role of H.B.I.C. Nonetheless, they respected Cameisha's intelligence and deferred to her when thinking was needed.

"You ok?" Aqua asked, seeing her friend conflicted by her thoughts.

"Yeah, I'm cool" Cameisha lied. Internally she was at war with herself. She was heading to do something that went against everything she was taught. Then again, she had been taught how to deal and kill so why not steal.

"Here, get this stuff in these sizes, Sincerity pays top dollar," Aqua advised as she handed her an order. Being a big girl she did well with the men's clothes.

"OK," she agreed, frowning at the foreign names on the list. Cameisha studied the list and put it in a pocket as the train pulled into the 34th street station.

They may have traveled in a group but once they entered the store it was each man for himself. The girls fanned out in search of high ticket items that would fetch a good price in the hood.

Cameisha found the high end boutique that held the items on her list. A can opener wasn't required her because these clothes didn't have security devices, they had security guards. The amateur thief stood out like a sore thumb to the trained security guard. She immediately keyed in on her as she shot her eyes in all directions.

After making direct eye contact with the plainclothes agent Cameisha began to load up. She had memorized the list and made quick work of hunting down the clothes. She tallied up the tag prices and was above a thousand dollars in hood prices when she turned to leave.

The security guard called other security guards as she followed Cameisha beginning to the exit. There was a nice little welcoming party waiting for her when she arrived.

Angle saw what was going down but was loaded with stolen gear herself and unable to warn her. Instead, she watched helplessly as she got apprehended.

"Come with us," one of the two agents said as they took Cameisha by the arms.

One look at the burly men dismissed the thought of making a break for it. Instead she dropped her head and let them lead her to the security desk.

Cameisha meekly obeyed and began pulling the stolen merchandise from her clothes. The Serge entered each price into an adding machine on his desk as she handed it over. A yellow smile spread on his weather beaten face when the tally reached over a grand.

"Ladies and gentleman we have a felony!" He announced to the delight of his underlings.

"What's your name girl?" The female officer demanded.

"Tyw… Cameisha." She stammered.

"I don't see her in here," the woman advised as she flipped through their list of known boosters.

"I better strip her sarge," the male guard announced lustfully. He had no idea how dangerous a proposition that was. Quite a few new thieves allowed him to strip search them out of fear. Cameisha was more afraid of being naked than going to jail.

"Let's not!" the sergeant frowned, "why are you stealing from my store!"

"I don't know sir," Cameisha admitted truthfully. She had no idea herself why she'ddid it. "I ain't never did it before."

"Well you got two choices, you can go to jail or call a parent to come pick you up," Serge offered. He lived long enough to tell bad kids from followers.

"Jail please," Cameisha replied to his surprise. No one he'd ever given the option to chose jail. That settled it for him.

"What's your phone number!" he barked as he picked up the old fashion phone on his desk.

An hour later Deidra stared down at her granddaughter like she had three heads, as the sergeant displayed the stolen loot on his desk. Cameisha couldn't bear to face her so she quietly sobbed looking down at her shoes.

"Officer pass me the two hundred dollar scarf so she can wipe her eyes," grandma said curtly.

"The fact that she would rather go to jail then face you shows me she knows better," Serge began. "I hope she has learned her lesson, have you?"

"Yes sir," Cameisha nodded, sounding every bit the country girl.

"I can pay for this stuff if you'd like," Deidra offered. She had the money but was relieved when he'd declined.

"That won't be necessary, just don't let it happen again or we will press charges!" He boomed.

"You don't have to worry about that," grandma assured him. Cameisha jumped up and fell in step behind her as she marched out. They were half way uptown before she finally spoke to the distraught girl.

"What did you learn today?" Deidra sighed. She was far more disappointed than angry. She knew what the cause of the problem was. She just hoped Cameisha did too.

"Not to be a follower," she replied proving that she did.

"Good!" grandma said emphatically. "I don't mind you having friends, you're young and need people your own age, but Cameisha those girls are temporary. Next year when you go to college they will be right there on that bench."

"I know grandma, I know," Cameisha assured her putting the incident behind them.

******

"Meisha! Ayo Meisha!" Aqua screamed from the courtyard. The sense of urgency in her voice made Cameisha abandon her studies to investigate.

"Oh snap!" she exclaimed as she saw what had them so excited. After pulling on a pair of sweat pants over her shorts she rushed down to the court yard.

"Sup girlie!" she exclaimed seeing Crystalline back on the scene. Then she noticed the wheelchair.

"Un,uh don't start frowning up on me now," Crystalline said seeing her reaction. "It's all good".

'It's all good' is a term that's known as an oxy-moron. People use it even when it's all bad. Dude blow trial and say 'the judge gave me twenty to life, but, it's all good'. The fuck it is.

"It is?" Cameisha frowned. She was still unfamiliar with the phrase.

"Hell yeah! I can still hit the blunt!" she laughed and snatched the weed from Zaria. "Plus I can't feel shit so them niggas with the big dicks can't hurt me."

"Ayo what's up with Tay and them?" Dasia asked to change the subject.

"My brother said they all got a year," Zaria replied.

"You see all these damn vultures," Dasia said pointing to the new faces milling around the projects. Dudes from Nelson Ave had walked the two blocks to set up shop since all the dealers were gone.

The girls spent most of the day on their bench catching up. The next week was spent there as well since Crystalline couldn't go anywhere. It was another week before they started leaving her there alone. It was summer after all and they could walk.

Chapter 24

"Man I wish I could go with y'all," Crystalline moaned as the crew smoked blunts in their pre-party warm-up. The music was too loud for them to hear the utter desperation in her voice.

To the girls credit they did attempt to bring her along a few times, but that wheel chair was too much work. Even the wheel chair equipped buses would speed past the stop so they wouldn't have to deal with it.

"Girl if you can't walk, you can't skate!" Zaria said not meaning it as harshly as it sounded.

The party at the Skate Key over in Harlem was the last Hoorah of the summer. School started next week and winter shortly after. This was it!

That's probably why Cameisha finally took the blunt when it was passed. She inhaled a big drag and held it like she had watched her friends do daily.

"OK, big girl shit!" Dasia cheered her on.

"Bout time your ass got down," Zaria co-signed Cameisha felt the warming glow seep through her system causing a smile to spread on her face. By the time they left the projects they all had a good buzz going. Crystalline did too, only she didn't have anywhere to go. As her friends caught a cab she rolled into the courtyard.

"Ayo what's good mama?" One of the renegades from Nelson asked as he took a seat on their bench. "You mind if I keep you company?"

"Only if you gonna spark that," she said looking at the blunt tucked behind his ear.

"This that grown man," he warned, letting her know the weed was laced. "They call me Mac by the way."

"Shit, I'm a grown woman," Crystalline shot back proudly.

"Alright, so let's slide in the stair case, let me see what you talking about."

"Let's roll," she joked and turned her chair towards the closest building. Mac got behind her and pushed her inside.

Crystalline heard the sizzle of the blunt when Mac lit it up and smelled the stench of the cocaine. She knew it was going too far, but it beat being alone. Once the wooly blunt was finished Mac had no problem getting inside of her mouth.

Blowing a strange dude was somewhat distasteful, pun intended, but at least she had some attention. Some affection and a friend.

******

The Skate Key was by definition a skating rink but no one really came to skate. Since the teens who frequented it were too young to get into the real clubs they turned the skating rink into one. The rink was now a dance floor except for a few kids circumnavigating on wheels.

Cameisha was giddy from her usual shot gun inhalation of weed and sips from Aqua's wine cooler. She still had finally hit the blunt directly. She would soon be smoking every time they hung out.

The weed smoke had loosened Cameisha's inhibitions to the point that a pair a Dasia's tight jeans didn't seem so bad. She surprised everyone including herself in the cute outfits. A skin tight designer T-shirt revealed a perfect set of round breasts that competed with what the tight jeans displayed.

Once her eyes adjusted to the artificial blue light of the skating rink Cameisha got another surprise.

"Are they doing my dance?" She exclaimed at the dance floor full of kids doing the 'fat-fat'. It was a highly embellished version now called the Mississippi,but at its root was the greasy burger.

The dance had spread throughout the five boroughs of New York City like a rumor. It even had a song and video dedicated to it. The girls feeling a sense of ownership, jealously rushed the dance floor to show them how it was done.

Cameisha got a great deal of attention when she began moving her curves to the music. Guys found a reason to gravitate in that direction for a closer inspection and girls hated her for it. Especially, Tovia.

"Ain't that, that country bitch you let beat you up?" she demanded to Lola. Lola flinched twice at the statement. One for calling the brutal girl a bitch, and again from the memory of the beating that came with it.

It was automatic. Like a package deal. Like burger and fries, or peanut butter and jelly. Except this was 'bitch' and beat down, fish and grits; automatic.

"That don't look like her," Lola lied. She really just wanted to have fun. Meet some guys get some numbers. Nowhere in her hopes for the evening did she include getting her ass whipped, again.

"Bitch let me find out you getting soft on me!" Tovia spat complete with spit. "Go get Sha and Ree-Ree."

Lola reluctantly gathered the rest of the girls from her projects. When they were all compiled they fell in beside thier commander and marched off to battle.

"Ayo look it!" Dasia warned with her normal theatrics. The two groups met in the center of the dance floor as innocents scrambled to get out of the way. The confrontation had 'brawl' written all over it.

"Bitch I don't appreci...

A left, right combo is what's known worldwide as a 'two piece'. A phrase had yet to coil the brutal onslaught that cut Tovia off.

Luckily, the tight jeans prevented Cameisha from kicking her, but the punches and elbows she took instead didn't make her feel so lucky. She felt woozy, sleepy, and nauseous, not lucky.

Lola snatched her away to prevent her from being pummeled any further. The move was taken as an act of aggression causing Zaria to swing. When she swung Ree-Ree swung, then Aqua swung, Sha swung and the melee was on.

With Tovia basically out on her feet the High Bridge girls easily whooped Bronx River Rats. This was what's meant by "win some, lose some."

Tovia didn't like to lose any. Once she shook the cob webs out of her brain she pulled a knife. A press of the shiny button flicked the switch blade open with deadly beauty.

Angle and Zaria were stomping Ree-Ree as if she had caught fire and they wanted to put her out. Cameisha saw the blade flash as she thrust it at Angles side. She yelled a shriek of warning that could not be heard over the commotion.

The long, slender blade entered Angles chest from the side. The cowardly, sneak attack, blind sided to be precise. It slipped between two ribs and burst her heart much like a pin would a balloon. She was dead instantly but her eye's fluttered as her brain adjusted to death. The shock of being newly deceased froze her in place for a few moments until nosey old gravity put its two cents in and pulled her to the ground.

No one wanted to be present at a murder scene when the cops arrived and the crowd dispersed accordingly. Angle's friends rushed to her side as her killer left with hers. A small hole in her shirt traced with large amounts of blood lied about the extent of her injury.

"Angel, Angel wake up ma!" Aqua demanded as she cradled her dead friend.

Cameisha, who had seen dead people before understood the faraway look in her eyes. There would be no waking up for their friend, not on this side anyway.

"Come on y'all we gotta bounce," Zaria warned as the sound of sirens grew closer.

"Go 'head, I ain't leaving her," Aqua insisted as she rocked the eternally sleeping girl. Not needing to be told twice they rushed from the rink. A block away they hailed a taxi for the ride across the bridge.

Once they made it back to High Bridge each girl rushed off to their own buildings seeking the safety and comfort that only 'home' could give you. They just missed Crystalline being wheeled back into the staircase with yet another intruder.

She was going downhill fast on her new set of wheels.

Chapter 25

The news of Angle's death spread so quickly throughout the projects that grandma knew what was keeping Cameisha in her room longer than usual that next morning. Hoping to ease the girl's pain Deidra began breakfast. Her efforts were halted by an empty egg carton.

"Aw shoot!" She grumbled just as Cameisha emerged.

"What's wrong grandma?" She inquired sincerely.

"Nothing baby, I'm about to run to the store for some eggs," came the reply.

"I'll go."

"No, get some rest. I heard about your friend. I'm sorry for your loss," Deidra said soothingly.

"I'm fine, I got it." Cameisha assured her and she went to put her shoes on before she could protest further.

The projects had the dark aura of death as Cameisha strolled through the court yard. Plenty of High Bridge residents had been murdered since she came to live here so she recognized the somber mood.

"Ayo ma! Come here mama!" One of the imported dealers called out from the bench they set up shop from.

Cameisha just frowned up and kept walking without even glancing in their direction.

"She think she all that," Crystalline said explaining the snub. She had become their unofficial mascot and her chair dubbed the 'head mobile'. Now that she began smoking laced blunts the door to degradation was wide open.

"You're the bitch who got bagged boosting my order?" Sincerity asked as Cameisha walked into the bodega. She glanced around the store and then behind her trying to locate the 'bitch'.

"Are you talking to me?" Cameisha asked getting heated. The word bitch was a trigger and just like any trigger it set off an explosion.

"Yeah I'm talking to you," Sincerity barked.

"My name ain't bitch, if'n you call me that again I'm finna' whoop yo ass," Cameisha stated plainly.

"Girl don't let that shit Karate Joe taught you go to your head!" She laughed at the threat. She may have found it amusing but didn't call her out of her name again.

"Karate Joe is my father. You ever even think about stepping to me and I'ma show you all the shit he ain't showed you!"

"Call me bitch again and you gone hafta' show me," Cameisha said not backing down an inch.

The two stared and studied each other for a few seconds that seemed much longer. It was like Kim Jung and Obama holding their nuts at each other. In the end they both decided that the eggs and juice they came for was a lot easier than Karate Joe-ing each other.

"Sorry about your girl. Angle was good people," Sincerity offered sliding in an inaudible apology.

"Thank you," Cameisha nodded accepting it.

"Fall through and smoke one Meisha," she invited over her shoulder as she left.

Cameisha was grinning from ear to ear from both the invite and that the diva knew her name.

"Ok!!!" she called out after her. She had yet another surprise waiting on her when she returned with the eggs.

"Oh, I almost forgot, you got mail," her grandmother said. Cameisha knew the woman well enough to know she wasn't feeling whoever it was from. She wasn't quite familiar with the government name written in chicken scratch but the jail stamp from Rikers Island she knew.

Cameisha knew the name from sharing classes with the sender if in name only. She smiled brightly as she took the letter, then rushed off to her room.

In the letter Tay showed off his illiteracy and bad grammar. She had to sit it down a few times to process what he might be trying to say. Through all the misspelled words and poor sentence structure he was proclaiming his love for her. It ended with the request to ride out the short bid with him.

"Of course I'll hold you down!" Cameisha cheered to the letter. Realizing he couldn't hear it ,she scribbled what would be the first of many letters back and forth.

After breakfast Cameisha decided to take Sincerity up on her offer to stop by. She slipped on a pair of sweat pants and pulled a t-shirt over her head. A small drop of blood on the sneakers she wore the night before caught her eye.

Tears warmed her face as the murder replayed in her mind. She selected another pair of sneakers but took the others along as well. She stopped by the trash compactor room and threw the evidence down the trash shute.

"What's good lil' mama?" Sincerity said cheerfully as she swung her door open to admit her guest.

"Chilin," Cameisha replied sounding like a New York native. She gazed around the spectacular project unit with awe.

The thick shag carpet gave the impression of walking in sand. All the walls were painted a pale blue to contrast the baby blue leather sectional that took up the entire front room. A sixty inch TV was mounted on the only wall not completely covered in mirrors.

Her unit also faced east which gave a clear view of the courtyard. The unlucky residents with units on the West had to deal with looking at the Hudson River, Manhattan and spectacular sun-sets. Noone but her cared about that. They wanted to see the courtyard so they wouldn't miss anything.

Peer pressure had led Cameisha to smoking weed almost daily now. Sincerity was not her peer so when she passed the blunt she took it. She hit the blunt exactly as her new mentor did even letting the smoke billow out of her mouth as she spoke as she did.

"Your girl is about to go out like a sucker," Sincerity stated plainly as she glanced out upon the court yard.

Cameisha turned to see who she meant and saw the visiting drug dealers doing wheelies with Crystalline's wheel chair. They propped her upon the bench while they took turns competing in the chair. She looked content as she pulled on a cocaine laced blunt.

"Yeah, I need to talk to her," Cameisha frowned.

"Girl, worry about yourself. You ain't from here and ain't gonna stay here. The rest of those girls are stuck. Three and four generations," she explained. "Some of this you take with you, some of it you'll leave here. Feel me?"

"I feel you," Cameisha lied. While it made sense it went against her earliest lessons. Back in Longs Mississippi neighbors helped each other. No man, woman or child was left behind.

For the next several hours Cameisha sat and absorbed all that Sincerity gave. The several blunts they shared made sure the information reached the deepest recesses of her brain so she could call on it when she needed it.

"So you ain't got no man?" The weed told Cameisha to ask.

"I guess," Sincerity answered wistfully. "Only he ain't the type of dude you can really have. I'm here for him whenever he decides to come around."

"And when is that?" Cameisha inquired, misreading vulnerability.

"Trust me, when dude comes through, you'll know it."

Chapter 26

"Ayo Crystalline! What the fuck!" Zaria demanded when the crew confronted their wayward friend in the courtyard alone.

"I'm chillin yo', doing me," she spat back with contempt.

"Chillin? Bitch you wildin!" Dasia corrected. Aqua still felt inferior and didn't speak while Cameisha didn't feel it was her place.

"Whatever," Crystalline said and lit a menthol.

"Bitch, Angle'sfuneral is today, you need to come on!" Zaria demanded.

"For real though," Dasia co-signed, "we'll take you on the train."

"I'll push and help you up the stairs," Aqua offered.

"Y'all bitches ain't wanna drag me along to no party and shit, but now y'all want me to come to a damn funeral! I ain't going to no graveyard but once in my life, and when I do, I ain't coming back!"

"That's that bullshit!" Dasia declared and stormed off. Zaria pursed her lips and shook her head with disgust before turning to leave.

Aqua and Cameisha fell in step behind them leaving Crystalline alone in the courtyard. She wasn't alone for long because not soon after, Rudy from Nelson Ave arrived on the scene. Seeing he had the girl all to himself he quickly rushed over.

"Ayo what's good ma, can you fuck?" He asked eagerly. The blow jobs were cool but he wanted to fuck.

"I mean I can, except I can't feel nothing," Crystalline replied. Had he cared he would have heard the obvious pain in her voice. He didn't, care that is.

"Shit, as long as I can feel it, it's all good." he announced selfishly. "I got a fat dime to hit."

Crystalline looked at the dime of crack in fear. She lived in a South Bronx housing project her whole life. She knew what happened when you crossed that line. Very few make it back from that place he was offering to take her. Even the ones who did manage to come back had still left a piece of them there. Usually, their dignity and parts of their souls.

"Bet, come on," she said pushing her chair across the line.

Once they got inside the stairwell Crystalline applied the handbrake that locked the wheels to her chair.

Rudy Picked her up and carried her to the landing between floors. He laid her down on the concrete and pulled her pants to her ankles. His pants dropped giving Crystalline a look at the dick she wouldn't get to feel.

Using spit for lubricant Rudy shoved himself inside of her. She could only watch as he humped and grunted.

"You telling me you can't feel this?" He asked pounding harder. He felt his dick would re-connect the severed nerves that left her dead from the waist down. Niggas!

"Yeah daddy that shit good," Crystalline offered.

"I know it," Rudy said proudly. He switched holes just to make sure she felt him, she didn't.

******

"This bitch here!" Zaria whispered bitterly as Angle's mother slinked in halfway through the service.

"What I miss?" She asked sitting in between Dasia and Cameisha. She smelled like weed and beer so Dasia turned her head to hold her tongue.

"How special Angle was," Cameisha gushed. She was too consumed with her thoughts to listen to what the preacher preached about.

"Angel was special!" her mother took to her feet and shouted. Cameisha reached up to steady her when she wobbled. "My Angle is an Angel!"

"Angle the Angel."

Once the service was over the girls piled into one of the vans the funeral home provided for the ride out to the cemetery. All the girls were now in tears as they watched their friend lowered into the hole. Angle's mother put on a show when she filed past to drop a rose on the casket. She did a mourning dance that resembled the Harlem shake.

"Oh shit!" she muttered as she lost her balance and tumbled into the hole.

"Somebody get that bitch." The preacher grumbled louder than he intended.

The solemn ride home was followed by a thick weed cloud. The rest of the summer passed quickly under similar weed clouds. It was a blur of weed, local parties and letters from Tay.

The next time they looked up it was time for school. Senior year!

"Really," grandma asked as Cameisha emerged from the department stores dressing room. She turned at an angle to inspect her backside in the mirror.

"Too much?" she asked cautiously. Looking cute had recently become an interest, only she didn't do it for show. Hanging out with Sincerity from time to time over the summer gave her an appreciation for clothes, but she still loathed the attention.

"In general I'd say no. Hell grandma got a pair of jeans that fit like that," Deidra replied.

"I better get the next size up," Cameisha advised herself then agreed with a nod.

"Good idea," grandma said proudly. She was delighted that the girl maintained her modesty, even if she really did own a pair of tight jeans herself.

"You know I could have paid for it myself," Cameisha said after the sale was completed.

"Your father left you that money for college. Besides, it's my pleasure." The mention of Cameron cast a somber mood over both the women.

The fog of despair hovered over them the whole way back uptown. It took the sight of someone else's misery to break the spell.

"Damn shame!" Deidra lamented at the sight of Crystalline rolling through the court yard drinking a 40 ounce bottle of Malt liquor.

"I swear I tried to help her," Cameisha moaned. It broke her heart watching her friend destroy herself.

It seemed she got worse every day. None of the other girls even spoke to her anymore. Now they openly scorned and ridiculed her as they would any other of the projects many junkies.

"Get yo' D.U.I ass away from here," Zaria barked when the wheel chair got too close to the bench she once ruled with an iron fist.

See, that's the thing about ruling. Either your subjects love you or hate you. If they love you they support and help you. Your success is their success. Go Team! But if they hate you, they'll follow and obey until they get a chance to kill you.

She felt the results of her tyrannical dictatorship as Zaria plunked her in the head with an empty juice carton. Only Aqua didn't laugh, she had a heart. A few girls who previously weren't allowed to come out because of Crystalline laughed as if it were funnier than it really was.

"Da-na-na-na-na-na-!" Crystalline cackled imitating the bat mobile as she rolled off in her head-mobile. The visiting drug dealers even had an emblem stuck on the back that read the same.

"Come on y'all," Cameisha pleaded as her and her grandmother passed by. "Give her a break?"

"A break! Shit my ass wasn't allowed to come outside for a year 'cause of that hoe!" Leslie spat. She was one of the pretty girls Crystalline tormented for being pretty.

"Chill y'all," Zaria ordered and the taunts came to a cease. Well, paused, because they would never really stop. Karma is funny that way.

******

First day of any school is always a big deal but multiply it by being senior year and it was really special. To be alive, free and still in school by 12th grade in the Bronx means you beat a lot of odds. They should give you a medal or something just for making it that far.

Cameisha was in front of the bathroom mirror admiring herself when Tovia came in to do the same. There was a brief tension filled pause when the enemies locked eyes.

Tovia was shocked but not scared. When no attack came she took it the wrong way. She thought Cameisha was scared.

"Tell ya' girl Angle I said what's up," she said with a smirk. "Oh...wait that's right, dead people can't hear."

"Remember you said that," Cameisha replied with a wicked grin. Her and her girls agreed to squash the feud before someone else got killed, but Meisha just had a slight change in plan. Tovia was dead first chance she got. Big mouth bitch just made a play date with death.

School was cool but Cameisha rushed to check the mail everyday.Most days she was rewarded by a letter from her boo. She and Tay had begun professing their undying love for each other. It was now serious. So serious in fact, that they made an appointment for her cherry.

Today in addition to the poorly written love letter she received, the correspondence she eagerly awaited. She jumped up and down hysterically as she read, and re-read the name in the left hand corner. Too excited to open it she ran upstairs to the apartment.

"What's wrong baby?" grandma asked startled by her rushing inside the apartment.

"It's from the school, the college!" she replied thrusting the letter at her.

"Ok thought you had beef. I was about to put my sneakers on!" Deidra said. Instead she pulled the reading glasses she wore around her neck onto her face. "Let's see here. The college of Atlanta is pleased to announce that you have been accepted into ..."

"Yes, yes, yes!" Cameisha said jumping up and down then launching into the 'fat-fat' dance. The original one not the souped up New York version.

"Congratulations baby, I'm very proud of you," Deidra gushed, spreading her arms. She let out a grunt as her granddaughter rushed in to accept the hug.

"I gotta go show Sincerity!" she yelled and disappeared from the apartment.

******

"That's what's up little mama! Proud of you chica," Sincerity gushed as she passed the acceptance letter back. "Told you, get up out of here and don't look back."

"Well I gotta look back 'cause of my girls, and me and Tay gonna get married. "

"Is that what he told you?" Sincerity laughed, "girl you too smart to be dumb"

"What's that mean?" Meisha asked earnestly.

"It means jail talk is different from real talk. It ain't exactly a lie, because them niggas be believing that shit themselves," she replied.

"Well, Tay aint like that. He might even come stay in Atlanta with me."

"Well, not. That lil' nigga was born in these projects and he gonna die in these projects. Only time he's gonna leave is for prison and come back, or leave for the graveyard and be gone forever. Leave here and don't look back." Sincerity urged. She hated not taking that advice herself many years ago. Now she only stayed because she had made a promise to her man to keep an eye on his people.

Cameisha heard the sincerity and regret in her voice and wanted to take heed, but, she was in love. You know how love does you? She pretended to agree as they smoked a blunt and changed the subject. The new subject was Crystalline.

"Damn shame," Sincerity exclaimed as she sped through the court yard in her chair. She was quite proficient now and could move at a pretty good clip.

She had to because her old crew would hurl objects and insults at her every time she flew pass. Neither of which bothered her now as the drugs and alcohol that she consumed either brought on or exasperated mental illness. The light was still on but nobody was home.

No one seemed to care other than Cameisha. Even Crystalline's mother would now walk past her without a word or a glance. Even when she had her son in tow they completely ignored the girl.

A few nights later Cameisha woke up in the middle of the night parched. "Man," she whined to herself seeing the glass she kept by her bed for this very purpose was empty. As she passed through the living room a commotion in the 'should have been deserted' courtyard, caught her eye.

A group of at least ten teenage boys came busting out of one of the staircases laughing. They were slapping five and carrying on loudly. The last of them was pushing the now lopsided wheel chair. When Cameisha saw it was empty she rushed to get dressed.

Cameisha ran to the abandoned wheel chair that the boy pushed into the center of the courtyard. All that remained was the white shoe lace Crystalline used to tie her weave to her head. Yeah ole girl was a mess. She darted into the staircase and there she was.

"Oh no!" she wailed as she found her friend on the landing between floors. Only the soft snores told her that the girl was alive, physically at least.

She was naked from the waist down and her shirt and bra pulled up to her neck. One glance at her round belly said she was three to four months pregnant. Actually the mis-shaped, malnourished monster in her belly was almost due.

Crystalline had semen on her body from head to toe. Globs ran from the battered vagina as well as swollen lips. Cameisha pondered for a second about smothering the girl to put her out of her misery. Put her down like they do at the dog pound.

She shook it off and decided to take her home. Now came the challenge of getting her dressed and into her chair. Cameisha kicked the filthy crusted panties away and struggled to get her grubby jeans onto her body. Once that was accomplished she went to retrieve the chair.

"Ayo Dexter, come help me," she called to a local junkie scouring the night for a hit.

"Ten bucks!" he exclaimed happily as he made his way over. Ten bucks was his going rate for any job. Wash your car, walk your dog, paint your apartment? Ten bucks!

"I got you, just come help me," she said leading him to her friend.

If touching all the semen bothered ole Dexter Cameisha couldn't tell. He hoisted her up and plopped her into the chair. He eased her down the half flight of steps and followed Cameisha to Crystalline's building.

"Who!" Crystalline's mother demanded at the knocks on the door. She snatched it open so forcefully one of her titties came free from her gown. She left it out."What you want me to do with that?"

"Fuck you mean?" Cameisha heard herself say. It worked and her mother sucked her teeth and stepped aside

"Just put her right there," Crystalline's mother said as soon as Dexter pushed her across the threshold.

Cameisha was hot, but satisfied that she was out of danger. She snarled at the women before turning on her heels. She made Dexter wait in the court yard as she went to retrieve his money. All she had was a twenty which meant he owed her an odd job.

Chapter 27

Even though Cameisha's influence led her wayward friends back to classes, as opposed to just going to school she was the only one who graduated on time. The rest of the crew was at least a year behind from fucking off the first couple years of high school. If they stuck to the example she gave they could get diplomas next year; except only they wouldn't.

For Cameisha, it was like aunt D.G. said 'a bad bitch is a smart bitch'. She was well on her way to becoming a 'Bad Bitch'. Just like Denise and her idol, Sincerity.

No matter what, her friends still traveled to the graduation ceremony and whooped and hollered when their girl crossed the stage. Not only was she the first, she would be the last. It was a joyous occasion and it only got better once they got back to the projects.

"Tay and them are home!" We-We said when he saw the girls exit a cab. We-we was called that because he was quick to pull his we-we out. I'm talking western, cowboy movie quick, like he had that guy in a special holster or something.

"That's what's up," Zaria said as they all turned their heads in case he exposed himself.

The girls posted up on their now seldom used bench and waited for the jail birds to come pluck, then fuck.

"I know Dee gonna want some pussy," Dasia said excitedly. They had been going together before he got knocked and had written each other the whole time. She knew when he was getting out and stopped fucking other dudes a month ago.

"Guess I'll let Rabbit hit," Zaria sighed as if it were a chore. These girls were the modern equivalent of women waiting on men to return from war. It was D-day. Dick day!

Aqua didn't say so, but she would just take whoever was left. She liked sex so it didn't feel like she was being used. Her girls had trained her to get something else besides dick out of the deal. A ten or twenty dollar, bag of weed, something.

Cameisha didn't say a word. True she had promised her virginity, or what was left of it to Tay, but it wouldn't be some rushed back seat or bent over in the stair case affair. No, grandma was going to Atlantic City for the weekend. They planned a romantic evening for the two of them.

Only problem was today was Tuesday and Tay couldn't wait until Friday for some ass. Careful not to shit where he ate he took his show on the road. He was boning all up and down the Grand Concourse. And of course they had more pressing matters to deal with.

******

"Ayo fam, we appreciate y'all keeping our seats warm while we was away but we home now," Tay told Mac and company. "Naw mean?"

"Kept y'all bitches warm too!" Mac laughed at the younger man.

"Damn sure did," Rudy co-signed. "Check it, we got this shit pumping so y'all lil' niggas fall back. Find somewhere else to play. Naw mean!"

"Word, word." Tay smiled and backed away. The dealers from Nelson laughed and mocked them assuming they had ran them off. They assumed wrong, it was just too early for gun play with the sun still up.

When Tay warned Cameisha to stay inside and out of the windows that night she knew something was going down. So of course she stayed in the window so she could see.

The first thing she saw was Crystalline being pushed home by her mother. She had been rushed to the hospital earlier to give birth, but came home empty handed. The fetus had died weeks ago and when the smell became too much her mother took her to have it removed.

"Ayo wheel her over here!" Mac called out. It must have sounded like Bernie Mac 'cause his crew doubled over in laughter. Cameisha was hot but was about to have a reason to smile herself.

She recognized her boyfriend by his swagger even in the hoodie and ski-mask. Dee and Rabbit were masked up too as they crept up from behind one of the buildings. The Nelson Ave Crew were still yucking it up when the first of what would be many gunshots rang out.

Cameisha couldn't help but laugh as Tay turned his pistol sideways and began dumping. Her grandfather told her only wangsters and movies heroes fired a gun sideways. It looked cool but no accuracy.

"I'm hit!" Mac yelled grabbing his ass cheek as he ran. Rudy didn't get to say anything as a lucky shot to the back of his head paid him back for the foul shit he did to Crystalline. Maybe they could put 'karma' on his headstone as well.

The rest of the crew scrambled away to safety. Luckily, Tay and company couldn't shoot and ran out of bullets. Cameisha mused to herself that if they staged a shooter behind the next building and one in the parking lot they would need more than just one body bag. Amateurs.

The heat from the murder drew heat so nobody could work the courtyard for a minute. The local precinct didn't mind the dealing; it was the murders they had an issue with. Paperwork and stuff. The lull was cool because Tay had an appointment with a vagina. A brand new one.

******

"So you ready?" Tay asked between tender kisses as he grinded himself between Cameisha legs.

"Mm, hm," she lied. Everything between opening the door for him and now laying naked was a blur. Her body was obviously ready as Tay lubricated himself with her fluids. She kept her eyes closed tightly so she wouldn't have to see it. The sight of a dick might have made her chicken out.

In fact she had chickened out the day before. She called herself doing research on sex and virgins and the results scared the shit out of her. The internet search led to a movie of a girl losing her cherry.

"Aw hell naw!" she cried out in fear when the man 'actor' dropped his pants. Not having much experience with penises she didn't know foot long dicks were a rarity in real life.

The sight of him pushing that pole into the screaming teen in the video haunted her. She could still see the blood when her eyes were closed. Had she watched another video or two she would have seen that same so called virgin getting hit in the ass. She had 30 movies under her belt already at 18.

"The hell wrong with you?" Zaria asked as Cameisha wondered over in a daze. She was still in shock from the carnage.

"Uh, nothing" she said shaking it off. Her mind was settled she wasn't doing it.

"What y'all talking about?"

"Dicks!" Aqua announced proudly.

"Danny got a big one."

"It's cool, not big as Calvin's," Dasia challenged.

"He can get around that corner," Zaria laughed.

They went on talking about everyone's dick size who passed. It seemed like they had fucked everyone male who passed by. Then Tay passed by. He winked as he rushed off to whatever he was doing.

The whole crew went mum and turned their heads like they didn't see him. Cameisha caught it and knew what it meant and asked, "well?"

"Tay got a little dick," Aqua cheered. "He cute though!"

"Yeah it's little," Dasia admitted.

"Tiny" Zaria co-signed with a frown. With that Cameisha changed her mind again. Tay was about to get him some booty.

"Hello?" Tay smiled from on top of Cameisha bringing her back to the present.

"I'm ready," she said answering the last question she heard before mentally leaving the building.

"Me too," he replied and began easing himself inside of her. Unfortunately, Tay did not really have a little dick. Her girls were fucking grown men and compared him to that.

"Owe!!" Cameisha hissed as she felt him sinking into her. "Easy, be easy."

He was. He gently stroked her virginity away. So much so, that there was almost a little pleasure with the searing pain. The fact that he didn't put on a condom was forgotten until Tay came inside of her with a grunt. She would have complained, if she wasn't so sleepy.

"What are you doing babe?" Cameisha asked as she awoke to find Tay rummaging through her closet.

"Nothing," he said scrambling to put back whatever it was that he was into. She remembered Grandma Deidra telling her that if you really want to get to your man, go through his shit while he was sleeping. She assumed that's what he was doing and smiled. 'He really wants to get to know me'.

"Ayo I gotta bounce. Got business," Tay said abruptly and pulled his jeans on as far as they went. For some odd reason they didn't go all the way up on his ass.

"K babe," I'm going to watch a movie with my girls so I'll see you later." She smiled to his back.

******

"Is our girl glowing?" Zaria laughed knowingly as they got seated in Cameisha's living room. Grandma would never allow the hood rats into her house so it was a first for all of them.

"I don't know what yall talking about," Cameisha giggled.

"Mm, hm!She done did the do!" Aqua said proudly.

"Ms. goodie two shoes got her some dick," Dasia joined in.

"So how was it?" Zaria asked like she cared.

"A lady doesn't kiss and tell so... that shit hurt like hell!" She laughed. "His thang aint small."

"It only hurts at first, you'll get used to it," Dasia said reassuringly.

"Yeah you gotta get broken in," Aqua said trying to help out. She didn't.

"Anyway....back to the movie," Cameisha said to divert the conversation off of her vagina.

"Anyway this movie is wack! What else you got?" Dasia scoffed.

"Go in my closet and pick something," Cameisha replied. "Anything but that damn PREACHERS WIFE! Still can't watch that trifling bitch!"

Dasia rushed off as Zaira lit a blunt and Aqua poured the wine coolers. Several minutes later she returned with CONFESSIONS OF A COLLEGE CALL GIRL. After the little party her friends helped clean up so no trace was left for grandma to discover. No such luck.

Chapter 28

"Hey grandma! Did you win?" Cameisha cheered as Deidra made it in the next day.

"Yeah I …," she paused, frowned and sniffed the air. " Mm hmpf! See you had that rat pack in here."

"I…um…I… you smell them?" Cameisha asked bewildered.

"Uh…yeah! I smell weave glue, bubblegum and cheap perfume! Oh and that weed y'all smoked in here," she answered frowning deeper. "I'm glad you'll be in college and away from those tramps!"

"I'm sorry grandma, we was just chillin'. I wanted to have company since I'm always at their house."

"It's cool." Grandma sighed. It's not like she forbid it and she disobeyed. "Just don't let it happen again."

The buddies spent a quiet evening at home talking and cooking. It would be the last quiet evening they had in a minute.

"What the What?" Cameisha asked frowning at the dishonorable discharge in her panties. Now, super clean the sight of dirty drawers troubled her. They only thing worse than it looked,was the smell. "Ugh!!"

"Grandma, what is this?" She asked throwing the panties at her. "It stinks too!"

"Cameisha are you having sex?" Deidra asked plainly.

"No, yes, just once," she rattled.

"Get dressed. We're going to the doctors," grandma said sadly. Now worried, Cameisha rushed to get dressed.

"Where are my keys?" She asked herself aloud as she searched her room. They were in none of the places they should have been. If not so concerned with her vagina she would have turned it upside down.

******

"The results are in!" The doctor smiled doing a bad talk show host imitation. The bad joke almost got him kicked in the teeth by Cameisha who was antsy to see what was wrong with her.

"Survey says ......gonorrhea! Ding, Ding, Ding!" he said, as if it were a joke. To him it was, all the niggers were either shooting or infecting each other. In fact his racist ass thought it was hilarious the way black people destroyed themselves. All they had to do is stand by and wait. Who needs the KKK when they eagerly killed themselves.

"Excuse me Meisha, turn your head while I beat his ass!" Deidra growled. The doctor having had his ass kicked before, in this same room, for that same joke, ran out of the room.

Grandma was mad at Cameisha too and wouldn't even look in her direction. A nurse came in to deliver the shot of penicillin that would cure the STD.She'd also taken another vial of blood and administered a pregnancy test.

Cameisha took it all in stride, solid as a rock, until they got inside the cab. No sooner did the taxi pull from the curb did the tears begin. The tears were closely followed by deep sobs and low wails.

"What have you learned?" Deidra asked softly.

"Use protection?" she guessed at the obvious.

"Well that too but," Deidra asked coaxed.

"Niggas ain't shit?" Cameisha said reliving her aunts admonition.

"Niggas ain't shit!" Grandma nodded. "So find a good man that deserves you. That boy ain't had that shit in jail, they check you for that. He caught it since he came home!"

Cameisha was 38 hot. She was through with Tay but wanted to kick his ass first. He stole her heart then broke it. The only thing that could be worse was if she was pregnant, or so she thought.

*****

"I know I locked my door?" Deidra said baffled at why it was unlocked when they returned her from the doctors. "Oh my!"

"The fuck?" Cameisha blurted as she stepped in behind her. The living room wasn't ransacked but it was touched. It was like someone was looking for what else they could take and not the primary lick.

Both women walked softly to the bedrooms and received the exact same shock. They had been hit up hard. Deidra looked at her jewelry box turned upside down and emptied. She had just inventoried it the night before when she returned from A.C.since her granddaughter had company over in her absence.

Cameisha's electronics sat right where she left them so her closet beckoned her. As soon as she pulled the door open she saw the empty sneaker box. Empty now, but had contained ten thousand dollars as well as some bank books her adopted father gave her. She never felt the need to hide them since she never had company. Until now.

"Dasia!" She fumed remembering sending her for DVDs. She didn't come back until half the blunt was gone. She must have lifted her keys as well.

"You finna' call the police?" Cameisha asked. Her accent had reverted a bit from the stress.

"No, I'ma find out who been in my shit and call somebody better than the police," Deidra spat hotly.

"I think I know. You ain't gotta call nobody. I'll handle this myself," Cameisha growled.

The tone said she could and would take care of it, but she was still gonna make the call.

******

"So what you gotta talk to me all in private, don't tell nobody about," Dasia asked as she let Cameisha in.

"Who's here?" She replied scanning the apartment.

"Nobody, but no homo," Dasia laughed at the half truth. She wasn't gay, just curious.

"Nah, nah, no homo," Meisha laughed a humorless chuckle.

"Ohh that sounds like Dee," Dasia said rushing to the window. That put her in the perfect position for the garrote Cameisha slipped out her pocket.

Her friend peeped out the window watching her on and off boyfriend as she put the cord around her neck. Luckily for all, something caught her attention just before she strangled the girl.

The sun had hit the slum diamonds in Tay's new medallion causing it to flash like a more expensive piece. The chain brought attention to the fresh cut and the new shirt over the new jeans atop the new sneakers. He was dead fresh for a broke nigga fresh out of jail.

"Girl what you doing?" Dasia asked swatting the killing device from her neck as if it were a gnat. Cameisha couldn't speak from the realization that Tay, not Dasia had robbed her.

"And my grandma!" she spat and marched out to confront him.

"Ayo I can't talk right now," Tay said dismissively as she approached assuming she was about to complain about him burning her. He actually planned to flip the script and say she burned him!

Cameisha had nothing to say instead she caught him with a jab that dropped him so fast that the hook that chased it missed. She kicked him in his head and moved over him to stomp him. He would have gotten beat to death if his boys didn't intervene.

"Get off my man!" Dee yelled and blindsided the girl with a vicious blow that knocked her down. Not wanting to be left out, Rabbit punched her too. Then Meech and Christian.

Tay shook off the near knockout blow and joined his friends attacking Cameisha. Every time they knocked her down she got back up fighting. Now she was in danger of getting beat to death. The boys kicked and punched her like a grown man as Dasia screamed for them to stop.

Cameisha was almost out when she saw Rabbit fall by a punch from Aqua who came to her aid. Now it was her who took a beating. A beating that saved her friend's life.

"Crazy ass bitches!" Tay spat, then spat on Cameisha as they left. Luckily they hit like bitches and nothing was broken or needed stitches. Paramedics treated them right there in the parking lot for their bumps and bruises, they were taken home for ice, aspirin and rest.

******

With the flow of drugs in the projects dried up, Crystalline was forced to stay sober and that was too much. Without her dope the voices in her head thundered commands. The more she ignored them the louder they got.

"Fine!" she said finally giving in. Her mother snapped her head in her direction and frowned.

Crystalline did what she was told and retrieved a length of rope from the closet. She sat it on her lap and rolled out of the apartment. She bypassed the elevator and dipped into the staircase.

She fastened one end of the rope around the pipe on the landing, just like instructed. The other end went around her neck. The voices had to coax her through tying the knot but she finally got it.

"Da-na-na-na-na-na-," she said as she flipped her chair on two wheels and launched herself forward. She sailed halfway down the steps until she hit the end of her rope, literally.

Crystalline's neck snapped so loud it could be heard several flights up. Her chair crashed at the bottom of the stairs creating more noise. The rest of the deaths that night would be quiet.

Like B.I.G. said; "bad boys move in silence and violence".

Chapter 29

Cameisha was devastated when she found out about Crystalline. The suicide barely caused a ripple in the fabric that was life in the projects. Police and the medical examiners people were in and out in minutes. Bagged up the corpse, not unlike one operates a 'pooper-scooper', and were out.

She was in far too much pain to sleep from the beating she took earlier so she lay emotionless in her bed. It hurt so much to move she barely breathed, just took sips of air.

Cameisha heard the front door open and close and soft footsteps go past her room. She smiled mischievously as she heard her grandmother speaking to a man. They conversed in hushed tones but she could tell it was a man. She was more respectful than nosey so she didn't strain to hear. As long as grandma's bed didn't start rocking she was cool.

She didn't recall going to sleep but figured she must have when she blinked morning into view. Still in great pain she loathed to move but her full bladder insisted. It was either get up or pee on herself. She gingerly rose to a seated position on her bed and saw it.

"Huh?" she questioned at the object on her dresser, that shouldn't be on her dresser. She pulled herself out of bed and went to get a closer look.

Sure enough it was the diamond chain and medallion Tay wore the day before. The one he purchased with the money he'd stolen from her closet. Even odder it sat atop ten bricks of compressed marijuana. Weighing by hand each brick was a pound. Under them were the bank books.

If Tay thought this would make up for what he did he was crazy. He shouldn't have stolen her stuff in the first place. And the beating! That was too much.

"Hmph!"Cameisha huffed as she scooped up the chain. Each step hurt worse than the last but she was determined to reach her destination.

She shuffled slowly down the hall and opened the door to the trash compactor room using her shoulder. She grunted and winced from the pain but kept going. After pulling the chute opened she tossed the chain inside and left.

After relieving herself Cameisha climbed back into bed. The plan was to go back to sleep but then she heard it. A deafening silence caused her to get up to investigate. She had never heard the bustling project this quiet. They hadn't been this quiet since 'He' was last here, but that was before her time.

"What in the world?" Cameisha asked as she looked out into the deserted court yard. It was empty. Completely still not even birds or squirrels could be seen running around.

Wanting to see for herself, Cameisha pulled on a pair of sweats and ventured out. She was the only one out.

"Hey Meisha–Meisha," Sincerity sang happier than Cameisha had ever seen her. Usually she's a boss bitch and fuck that, fuck her, fuck you. Today she's Mary Poppins.

"Fuck got into you," Cameisha frowned as she entered her apartment.

"Some good dick!"She gushed girlishly and actually giggled.

"Some dick? I thought you said you had a man?" Cameisha questioned.

"I do, and he came to see me last night and laid pipe!"

"I thought I had one, 'til he stole my money and whopped my ass," Cameisha whined. "That was my college money, what I'm 'posed to do now?"

"Wells Ms. Ceily..." Sincerity teased at the re-emergence of her southern accent. "Sell the weed mama. Ten pounds will make ten stacks and then some."

"Yeah I guess I could 'cause... wait! How you know about the weed?"

"My man told me," she replied coyly. "Now get home before all the drama starts."

Cameisha didn't ask who this mysterious man was or what drama she was referring to. Instead she took her advice and went home. She found out what the drama was shortly after getting inside.

One by one project buildings became crime scenes as bodies were discovered. First Rabbit's mother walked into his room and saw his brain had fell-out of the large hole in his head. At first glance, it looked like a suicide, where he put a gun in his mouth and fired, but there was no gun. Nor did his family hear any shots.

No one heard any shots, yet they were all dead. Rabbit, Dee, Tay and two more of his crew that either took part, or watched Cameisha get beat up.

"Baby get out that window before the police wanna come up here and ask a million questions," Deidra said as she breezed through the living room.

"Don't want that," Cameisha said ducking out of sight. She quickly noticed two things about her grandmother. The first was her demeanor. She was so happy, she was humming an Al Green song. The second thing she noticed was that she was wearing her jewelry;the jewels that were stolen from the apartment a couple of days ago.

"Grandma you got your stuff back!" she cheered at the sight of the pretty pieces.

"My grandson came last night! He got them for me," she said proudly. "I wanted you to meet him but it was late, and he had a lot of work to do. Probably went to see that girl too no doubt."

That's when Cameisha put it all together. Killa was here!

******

News of the murders spread quickly, and again the Nelson Ave crew came back to fill the void. Cameisha convinced her girls to sell dime bags for 3 bucks off each sack. She bagged up sixteen hundred off a pound and supplied the girls. This way she could make her ten grand back and not get her hands dirty.

Only problem was, Mac and his crew had already established themselves. All the customers went to them rather than the girls. Zaria was the one who came up with a sales plan that worked instantly. She rushed upstairs to put it in motion.

"Now watch this!" Zaria said when she returned wearing a tiny pair of shorts and wife beater. Not a single man walked past. Even dudes, who didn't smoke, bought weed so they would have an excuse to talk to her.

Of course Dasia got the same results, Aqua not so much. Mac felt the pinch in his pocket, and stepped to them.

"Ayo check this, I don't mind y'all being out here looking cute. Well, you cute, you 'aight, and you.... Anyway, y'all bitches beat it. This is me! Don't get hurt," he said.

"What?" Cameisha asked in disbelief when her girls ran to her with the news. "See that's that shit I hate! Niggas wanna hog the block! Where I come from hogs get slaughtered!"

She was about to get her hands dirty!

******

The crew wasn't too pleased to attend Crystalline's funeral, but Cameisha insisted. Since she was the one with the work she was now in charge. They griped and moped all the way up town to Woodlawn Cemetery.

"Still don't see why we gotta go...We ain't even fuck with her no more," Zaria pouted. It was clear she was upset about being bumped from the head of the pack.

"For real though! She was a damn crack head," Dasia seconded. Cameisha didn't hear them as she watched the city streets rush below from the elevated train.

New York was crazy, wild and exciting and she loved it. She also missed the peace and tranquility of her rural roots. In a few months she would be headed south to attend school in Atlanta. The time couldn't come quick enough.

"Yo' we here Meisha," Aqua said gently pulling her back to the present. The worst part of someone pulling you out of your head is when it's done abruptly.

A short cab ride later they entered the same funeral home, where they attended Angle's funeral, almost a year before. Only this time they were completely alone, the place was empty.

"What the fuck yo'!Where her people at?" Zaria complained loudly. Cameisha was really getting tired of her, but this was neither the time nor the place.

Besides, she wondered the same thing. Where were her people, her mom, sisters, her son? Not a soul showed up to see the girl off. She led the way up to the casket so they could say their good-byes.

"The fuck!" Dasia wailed at the sight of the body in the cheap casket. Cameisha even felt her knees buckle looking down at her.

Crystallinelooked more like an avatar than a human. She even had a blue-green tint to her skin. Her face was mis-shaped from the abuse she suffered in the last year of her life.

Aqua couldn't take it and ran away crying from the parlor. Zaria sucked her teeth and walked off, and Meisha reached down and touched her cold hand.

"Ayo how long y'all staying up here? I'm 'bout to bounce!" Zaria demanded. She didn't wait for a response before storming off.

"Go get Aqua, y'all go on back to the projects. I'll catch y'all at home." Cameisha said still unable to take her eyes off the dead girl in the box.

"Excuse me miss? Miss? We're about to close," the funeral director advised gently. Cameisha was still holding the dead girl's hands an hour later. Her mind had traveled around the globe and back. She took a deep breath that exhaled as a sigh.

It was time to go. It was time for her to put someone in a box.

******

"You straight yo'?" Zaria asked, as Cameisha returned to the projects.

"Yeah I'm cool," she replied with what could be considered a smile. She realized the act of contrition was as close to an apology as it was going to get and she accepted it.

"What them niggas talking about?" Meisha asked pointing at Mac with her head.

"Some bull-shit!" Dasia pouted. "Talking 'bout if he see us sell a seed he gone put his foot in our ass."

"Sho-nuff? Well y'all go get some rest tonight 'cause we back to work tomorrow!" Cameisha proclaimed. Her crew didn't doubt her one bit and jumped up to comply.

When Cameisha got upstairs grandma Deidra was waiting on her. In her hands were the lab results from her tests at the hospital. She sank down in a chair and stared at it.

"Well?" grandma said, as she tore into it. Her eyes scanned the lines but her face gave no clue one way or the other. She sighed as she folded the letter up and put it back into the envelope. "You're not pregnant."

"You don't seem too happy," Meisha noted.

"I'm not. I'm very upset you did this to yourself. It could have been so much worse. Cameisha, I love you girl and I will protect you from any and everything, except you. I cannot protect you from you."

******

The plan was simple and if it came off as planned, it would rid the projects of the intruders. The plan was simple and if it came off as planned, it would rid the projects of the intruders. A Glock 23 was exactly where her grandfather left it in case she needed it. Cameisha needed it.

She was fond of the small 40 Caliber pistol that fit nicely in her hands, but could stop a truck. This was her weapon of choice at the range and she was deadly accurate with it.

Mac and his crew were the only ones not in the court yard. That meant no witnesses or bystanders. Cameisha crept from behind the building and took aim. She pointed the large caliber gun at the back of Mac's head and began slowly squeezing the trigger.

"What the fuck!" Mac yelled as the forty in his hand exploded. Cameisha emptied her clip making sure to only hit the bench and their beer bottles.

When they had taken off running so did she. She put another clip in as she ran around the building to cut them off. She fired on them again making it look like they were surrounded. This time Meisha couldn't help herself. She took aim and shot Mac dead in his ass.

She got a big kick watching him hop and scream from not knowing which way to run. They put their hands in the air and laid down. That's where the police found them when they finally responded to the shots fired call. They all had dope on them and got cuffed and carted away. The girls now had the trap to themselves.

Chapter 30

Cameisha watched proudly as her girl's pumped dimes of weed. She wasn't just watching them, but police and jackers also. The walkie-talkie was to alert the crew if po-po showed up, while a throw away 380, tucked in the garbage was for the jackers.

"Look at you mama," Sincerity laughed as she and her son walked through the court yard. Little X as he was called ran for a smooch and then back to his mother.

"Just wanna get my college money back. That's all" Cameisha said believing it. "No telling how long it will take to move all that weed and get my ten grand."

"You gonna make ten thousand and stop? Quit? Fuck outta here!" Sincerity laughed.

"I'm for real! If dude ain't rob me I wouldn't even have to do this! All I want is my money back."

"Bet a stack?" she dared.

"A grand that I won't quit once I finish the pack?Bet!"Cameisha exclaimed. "Shoot that will make eleven G's to go to Atlanta with."

"Excuse me, we done," Aqua interrupted. Zaria and Dasia were close behind.

"Done what?" Meisha asked confused.

"With the pack, it's all gone," Zaria replied.

"Y'all sold a hundred and fifty bags already!"

She asked looking at her watch. Only three hours had elapsed.

Zaria's sales pitch of dressing half naked or half-dressed was obviously working. Dudes from all over High Bridge came through to holler at the cuties; and Aqua too.

Cameisha gave them each more dime bags after collecting three hundred and fifty from the first package. She was at 1/10th of her goal. By the time they wrapped up for the day she was even closer.

The Dope girl had learned from the Dope boy and knew what days and times sales were brisk, compared to down times. She maximized the up-swings and was done in a week.

"Owe this girl a damn stack," she admitted to herself. Sincerity was right.She was going to keep hustling. Just one more flip, just once more.

Once the word was out about the fat bags of good weed the second flip took six days. Taking a lesson from her father's play book she dubbed her product 'fat-fat'. The marketing worked and err'-body wanted some of that 'fat-fat'. It even made it into a verse of a rap song.

'Keep a burner in my back-pack smoking on the 'fat-fat'.

******

"I hate to say I told you so but..." Sincerity laughed as Cameisha bagged up at her apartment. She had just re-upped spending five grand on ten pounds and had close to ten grand saved.

"No you don't 'cause you made a stack of that told you so" Cameisha quipped.

She was making mo-money so she should not have been surprised when she had mo-problems.

"Ayo Z, this short. This is only three ten," Cameisha said after a second recount.

"Word?" Zaria frowned as if shocked. "I think my moms hit me up. She be buggin'!"

"Aight yo', just make it up on the next pack," she said dubiously.

This wasn't the first time she was short. Usually it's five or ten bucks so it gets over looked, but forty. Funny, that her moms hitting her up didn't stop her from buying the new sneakers on her feet.

Once the next package was done, they all went down to Fordham Rd and did some shopping. Cameisha already had all of her clothes for college, but a chic could never have too many clothes.

Cameisha's money was a little longer than her friends so she was able to shop long after they were spent out. No one seemed to mind except Zaria. No one seemed to catch it except Cameisha. Her father told her this would happen.

"Ayo check," Meisha began as they took a cab back to High Bridge. "If y'all invest y'all money back into the next pack, y'all could make a lot more money."

"Shit, I'm cool Dasia shot back immediately. I mean it ain't as much as boosting but it's mad easy! I'm cool"

"Me too," Aqua said. The two to three hundred dollars a day she made was way more than she could possibly eat.

"Shit why you don't just split the pie four ways? Since you so concerned about our pockets," Zaria announced.

Now, the proper response would have been to tell the driver to stop, get out and beat Zaria's ass. Instead she said "That's what's up."

Cameisha was sitting on close to twenty grand, twice what she came for. Besides she was leaving soon and leaving the ball rolling would help them once she was gone.

"Ok, I'll put up the money and we split it four ways. Only one rule. Whoever comes short gets their ass whooped by the rest of the crew. A second for every dollar short," Cameisha added. This way Zaria could buy an ass whooping with her stolen money.

"Bet, bet, that's a bet," they agreed one by one. Guess who was last to agree?

Cameisha kept her word and invested her profits into a package for the crew. They stood to make four thousand dollars apiece if they all kept it one hundred. They didn't.

"Ayo my moms got me again. I'ma hafta' make mines up on the next flip," Zaria explained nonchalantly.

"You mean you ain't got shit on the next flip!" Dasia demanded.

"Naw yo', I'll catch up on the next one," she said fingering her new gold hoop earrings.

"Yo', lets not talk business out here in public lets go up on the roof," Cameisha suggested. This was the place she had learned to fight.

"Shit bet!" Zaria said hearing and accepting the challenge, she led the way marching into the building and banging on the elevator like she was in a hurry.

"Ayo two stacks, that's like ....an hour," Dasia said calculating the beating time.

"Thirty three point three minutes," Cameisha said calculating a rough guess.

"Hope you bitches can hang that long!" Zaria said confidently. She knew she had skills with the hands. "Let's get it!"

As soon as the girls reached the roof-top Zaria bombed on Meisha. She intended to follow the blow up with a second, but a body blow from Aqua lifted her off her feet. Dasia joined in throwing dainty little punches. Cameisha shook off the blow and joined the fray.

Aqua knocked her down and the girls moved in and began kicking and stomping her. Zaria never quit or cowered.Instead ,she was still talking shit and fighting back. That's when Cameisha had an epiphany.

She suddenly stopped kicking and walked away. Aqua and Dasia stopped too and wondered what was going on. Zaria still had thirty minutes left.

"Where you going yo'?"Dasia asked.

Zaria took advantage of the lull and jumped to her feet. She pulled a straight razor and took a swing at Dasia's face. The blade was so sharp she didn't even know she was hit. A split second later a white line appeared from Dasia's forehead, through her eye, ending on her cheek. The line turned red and began gushing blood.

Zaria wasn't done yet. She turned and swung the super sharp blade at Aqua. Aqua reacted with a move Cameisha had taught her and kicked Zaria square in her chest. The blow sent her reeling backwards ten steps. The only problem was she was only seven steps from the edge of the roof.

Nobody moved until they heard the 'thud' of Zaria's body reaching the ground below. Thinking quick, Cameisha acted immediately. It was like her grandfather said; panic and die or think and survive.

"Yo' Dasia, you stay here! When po-po come, just say some niggas tried to rape y'all, y'all fought, you got cut and she got pushed," she demanded. "You follow me?"

Dasia nodded holding her face with blood practically squirting between her fingers. Cameisha took all eleven flights of stairs two at a time with Aqua close on her heels. They rushed out the back of the building, around front and joined the growing crowd.

Cameisha could only shake her head at the mangled mess that she once considered a friend. She was bent and twisted from the fall, but her earrings were cute.

"Oh I'm so sorry!" Rosa wailed and embraced Meisha tightly. This reminded her that she was supposed to be upset and grieving. Appropriately, she began to weep.

Aqua looked confused, which was about right for Aqua. It took a second but she caught on and began crying as well. Dasia too put on an Oscar worthy performance. When they brought her down she was wailing and heaving as they led her away in an ambulance.

******

The tears that ran down Cameisha's face as she attended the third funeral were as real as the pain in her chest. This was definitely one of the 'downs' of the ups and downs of life.

"I'm done y'all. I can't do it anymore," Cameisha whispered to her friends seated beside her in the funeral parlor. "I'm finna' go to school in two weeks; it's over."

"What about us? You just gonna leave us?" Aqua asked sadly, as Dasia touched the bandage covering her stitches.

"I gotta go ma, but I'll come get you one day. That's my word," she vowed, meaning every word of it. These two survivors were considered the weak ones, the followers, but they'd survived. They survived because they were loyal.

"Go on and do you chica. We gone be aight," Dasia offered. She didn't know how true it was but she didn't want to hold her friend back.

"We can go down to Atlanta and sell weed!" Aqua cheered, way too loudly for a funeral.

"No. No more drugs for me," Cameisha shot back. The words of her father came rushing into her head when she said it.

'That's the thing about hustling, it's an addiction. Once you start you can never really stop. Take breaks maybe, try something legit but you'll be back.'

"No daddy," she replied to the inaudible warning causing her friends to look at her oddly. "I'm finna' go to college, no more Dope Girl."

The End.

Epilogue

"Shit!!!" Jackie screamed as an orgasm wracked her curvy black body. Her lover Joline just sucked a nut out of her swollen vagina.

"You like that?" Joline asked proudly, still glistening in the spray Jackie emitted when she came.

"Loved it daddy, I'm gonna miss that tongue," she lied. Jackie wasn't even a lesbian but thought it wise to hook up with the stud to do her little bid. It was a matter of survival. She was no punk though, in fact she was a killer. She had just murdered her exboy friend the notorious Ill-Will. She was the other half of the deadly stick up kids called Jack and Ill.

The D.A. refused to charge her on the murder, calling it self-defense. The dirty 380. She used to do it was a different story. Jackie copped out to two years on a gun charge, two years ago. It was time to go home.

Jackie vowed to never step foot into her projects again. It was full of murderous memories and domestic abuse. She was done. Having been accepted to numerous colleges and universities she had her pick of a dozen schools throughout the country.

It was fate and good writing skills by the author that she chose the same Atlanta College. Yep, same school Cameisha was going to.

Jackie from Jack and Ill meets the Dope Girl! I can't wait for part two!

Also available now,

SEX AND VIOLENCE:

CHAPTER 1

"Um, excuse me mommy. Can I talk to you?" Triste asked timidly. She knew her mother didn't like being disturbed while she was either watching her soaps or smoking her blunts. She just so happened to be doing both at the present time.

"Shit, you already talkin' to me, you stupid, yellow heifer! Fuck you want now!" Her mother barked viciously while exhaling a plume of putrid weed smoke in the eleven year olds face.

"It never fails, as soon as I light up my kush, your ass got something to damn talk about!" The statement was true, since the woman was always smoking. It was near impossible to find a time when she wasn't high, or getting high. Triste took a deep breath to summon her strength and began to speak. "It's about Joe," she stammered. She knew her desperate over weight mother loved her no good boyfriend desperately; as far as she was concerned, he could do no wrong.

"What about him?" she demanded bolting up in her chair. Triste was so scared she almost abandoned the mission to take off running instead. It had taken a week to build up the courage, so she refused to back down now. She was no punk in the streets and wouldn't be one in her own home; besides, it was her body.

"He's been touching me!" she announced triumphantly. It felt as if the weight of the world had been lifted off of her shoulders. "He's been feeling on my breast and my booty!"

" Breasts'! Booty! Bitch, you ain't got no damn breast or no damn booty! Why the fuck would my man wanna touch your nubs or your narrow ass, when he's got all this?" she laughed.

"See, that's why I can't stand your little yellow ass! Always thinkin' you so pretty; my hair, my eyes… fuck you and your long hair and blue eyes! Bitch I'll cut that shit off and pluck them shits right out of your big ass head!" She spent the next ten minutes berating the child until Joe walked in. It was one of those classic 'speak of the devil' moments.

"What y'all talkin' about?" he asked of the animated conversation. "Well, perhaps the word 'conversation' was too mild a word to use to describe their dialogue. This was pure verbal child abuse; cruelty to a child. He could tell from the scowl on the little girl's face that she'd told on him.

Joe knew he gone too far by finally moving up to touching the child. For months, he had settled for just admiring her; stealing peeks when he could.

Triste's father was a white man, which accounted for her golden skin type and her good hair. She had a headful of curly, light brown hair that extended to the middle of her back when pulled straight. Throw in the eerie set of pale green eyes, and she was destined to be a drop dead gorgeous woman one day.

One day…. only Joe didn't want to wait that long.

Like most child molesters, he had started off slow; sodomite foreplay. He was content with staring at the frail child whenever he could. Then, he'd gone to looking up her dress while she watched TV; the Power Puff Girls on her panties had a new fan. Next, he began to 'accidently' walk in on her at bath time. Of course, there was the usual pedophile past time of sniffing her panties and masturbating on them. He would take it out sexually on her mother whenever he'd get too worked up.

Janice had noticed the sex had gotten better but she didn't know why. Mentally, and in Joe's sick mind, he was fucking her daughter.

"This little frail bitch, who thinks she soooo pretty, tryna' tell me, you been touchin' her bony lil' ass! Tell her that's a damn lie!" she demanded.

"Uh, it's a lie," he repeated without conviction. He thought the gig was up, until she'd given him a way out. Had she looked up through the weed smoke, she would have seen the guilty look on his face.

"I knew it!" Janice cheered like she'd won a prize. "I knew your trifling ass was lying! Ain't nobody touchin' your ass! You better not never tell me nothin' else 'bout my man! Now get your narrow ass out of here before 'I' touch your ass!"

The stupid woman had just given him the green light to rape her daughter; if she couldn't turn to her, her own mother, who could she turn to?

* * * * * *

"I don't know why I'm so tired," Janice yawned at the dinner table. She was bobbing her head like her weave was too

heavy, in an effort to stay awake. "You look tired," Joe
agreed. He didn't say anything about the GHB he'd slipped in
her Malt liquor. He'd started to drug the child too to make her
more pliable, but what fun would that be?

Triste inherited her unknown father's above average
IQ, and she knew something was out of order. She had
watched her mom drink and smoke for years, and had never
seen her fall asleep at the table. The lustful looks Joe shot
across the table at her, terrified her. She shoved the last few
bites of food into her mouth and fled to her room.

Joe was in no hurry. He got up and began to drag his
drugged up girlfriend to the room they shared, and lifted her
big ass onto the bed. He then took a quick shower, brushed his
teeth, and then, brushed his waves for his date; his 'booty
call'. He was rock hard when he walked down the hall to
Tristes' room. Since it was technically rape, he didn't bother
knocking; he just used a shoulder to bypass the flimsy lock,
and in he was in.

"Please, Joe," Triste pleaded, cowering beneath her
pink Power Puff comforter, as if it were a shield. The multiple
of layers of clothing she'd donned were her armor. The winter
coat, house coat, two layers of pants, shorts and long johns,
only prevented the rape for as long as it'd take Joe to get them
peeled off of her.

"Girl, what you fighting for? You know you want
this," he said seductively. In his sick mind, she was playing
hard to get. Triste was so scared, she'd peed on herself. Joe
didn't care. He played in the stream of urine with his fingers.
Once her bladder was empty, he leaned in and sodomized her.
She had no idea what he was doing down there or why, but

prayed it would soon stop. It didn't and his finger only made it worse.

"Oh, so you a virgin, huh?" Joe exclaimed at the blood on his finger. The discovery would've been remarkable, had she been twenty-one, instead of eleven. Hell, in the inner city, keeping your cherry until the age of sixteen was doing good.

Triste didn't reply. When she saw the bloody finger, she didn't panic. She took a deep breath and began to fight. She lifted one of her straw thin legs and kicked him as hard as she could. The blow didn't hurt him, but moved him enough for her to stand. She had always been a vicious little fighter in school and around the hood with girls her own age, but Joe was a grown ass man; she was no competition for him at all. She fought with everything she had, but, to no avail. The tiny blows bounced off like bullets would do from Superman's chest. Joe smiled, took the beating in stride, and lay back down.

"Hush up all that screaming now girl," he said cupping a hand over her mouth. The large hand covered so much of her face, that it had blocked her nose too. Triste was on the verge of blacking out before he'd finally removed it. "Open that mouth again, and I'ma put this dick in it."

The threat did the trick and she shut her mouth tightly; no way did she want him to do that. She'd once made the grim mistake of peeking into her mother's cracked bedroom door and had watched as Joe put the whole thing in her mother's mouth. Curiosity and fascination had caused her to stay and watch her mother give him a blow-job. She already knew how that had ended; no thank- you, she would pass on that.

Joe used his full weight to hold the child in place and, then, he raped her. Despite the threat of Triste screaming her lungs out from the pain of being invaded, Joe finished with a grunt, rested and, went at it again; this assault went on all night.

******

"Fuck wrong wit' you!" Janice demanded when she saw her daughter limping the morning after the rape.

"He….I 'um….I fell off my….twisted my," she said scrambling to come up with a lie. Good thing Janice didn't really care what was wrong and didn't really listen to her response.

Joe cracked a sly smile to see that Triste was unable to tell her mother about the rape. He'd gotten hard just thinking about his new arrangement; for him, dark couldn't come soon enough so he could do it again.

"Clumsy ass little heifer, you make me sick!" Janice chided bitterly. She really loathed her daughter. It was a jealousy- hate, fueled by hearing the words 'oh, she's so pretty, or 'is she Indian' and 'look at her eyes…look at her hair'. Being a hater was one thing, but to hate on your own kid, took it to a new low.

Triste was too sore for panties, so she dressed gingerly in a pair of sweat pants. She had balled her blood and semen crusted bed sheet to toss into the apartment dumpster on the way to school.

"Girl, what's wrong with you?" Triste's best friend Jasmine asked.

"My momma's boyfriend raped me!" she spat bitterly. Being able to finally admit it was a relief, and caused tears to stream from her eyes; she was far more angry than sad.

"He did what? Girl, we need to kill him!" Jasmine yelled. "My brother got a lot of guns; we can easily get one.

"If he touches me again, I'ma kill him," Triste vowed.

"What your momma say?"

"She ain't say shit, ain't wanna hear nothing 'bout her man," she said mocking her mother.

"Ok, we can steal one of his guns when we come home from school. Oh shit! There goes Kenya!"

Kenya was the Joker to Triste's Batman. They were arch enemies since first grade. They had been beefing for so long, that they'd both long forgot why they were even fighting, but fight did they, almost daily.

One reason they fought was envy. Kenya was black and ugly, to Triste's light and pretty. Triste's hair was long and curly, while Kenya's was 'Th' long; no typo, it was just long enough to spell 'that'.

Both girls instinctively looked down to make sure their Tennis shoes were tied tightly for battle. Sometimes, the girls traded insults as a prelude to a fight while other times they fought on-sight; this was one of the 'other times' and the girls had attacked.

Fights between the girls were usually even matched. Some days Kenya won and some days, Triste would come out on top. Today with Triste's added rage, Kenya didn't stand a chance. Triste was whooping her all the way up Martin Luther King Blvd. Kenya didn't have a dream, she was having a nightmare. They fought until they'd reached the front of the school.

Kenya landed a wild kick to Triste's sore vagina and changed the tide of the fight. When she doubled over in pain, Kenya got on her ass. There were several teachers amongst the fight fams, luckily one of them was matured enough to break it up.

"You two, again!" Mrs. Rangle yelled pulling the girls apart. These same two combatants accounted for a quarter of the school's fights. "What are the two of you fighting about now?"

Both girls stared at each other, while waiting on the other to answer. Neither had a clue, they certainly couldn't verbalize the fact that their stressful, deprived upbringings had left them both angry and desperate. They couldn't explain how the verbal abuse, physical and now, sexual abuse, made them want to lash out at something or someone. So, instead they fumed "she started it!" They'd both yelled it out at the same exact time. "No, she did!"

"Child, you're bleeding!" The teacher exclaimed at the sight of blood between Triste's legs.

"Are you on your period"? "No!" She replied immediately, not knowing that she really was for the first time. She initially thought it was from the rape. She knew if she couldn't tell her mother, she damn sure couldn't tell a teacher. All black children knew better than to tell anybody what was going on in their houses. The ghetto had a rule book, and that rule was in it; "Rule #12- DON'T TELL WHAT HAPPENS IN MY HOUSE.

"The heck you're not!" Come on here girl!" she demanded and pulled her to the nurse's office. "You don't have any pads young lady?"

"I have a writing tablet," Triste responded, confused by what was going on.

"Got another one," Mrs. Rangle told the nurse as she dragged her in by the arm. "Get cleaned up, I'll go get you something to wear."

Triste had finally figured out what was going on, when the nurse handed her a sanitary napkin, sometimes called a pad. She went into the bathroom and pulled off her soiled clothing. Being sore and swollen made that task much more difficult than it actually should have been. By the time Mrs. Rangle returned, she had cleaned up as best she could.

"Umph, these should fit you," she said handing her a pair of panties and a pair of pants from the lost and found. The old clothing fared a lot better than some of the ghetto kids who had been lost, but never found. The way Triste had looked curiously at the pad, made it obvious that she didn't know how to use it; she wasn't the only one though. Plenty of the young girls whose mothers were too busy drinking or playing Spades to properly care for their daughters, had rushed in the nurse's office screaming for an ambulance at the arrival of their first period.

"Girl, here!" Mrs. Rangle huffed, taking the pad. Triste watched her demonstrate how to use it, and then, she got dressed.

"Triste got her period y'all!" Kenya yelled, when she walked into the classroom. The class erupted into jeers and laughter; even though most of the girls, including Kenya, had already begun menstruation. When someone teased you, you had to laugh along with them; whether it was funny or not - 'Ghetto Rule Book #87'.

You already know Triste couldn't stand the teasing. She marched straight over, and bombarded her. Kenya had no choice, but to take another beating. This was their second fight of the morning, and it had gotten them both sent home for the rest of the day.

Since Joe didn't work a conventional job, Triste decided instead of going home, she would rather roam the streets of South West Atlanta until school let out, that way she could wait with Jasmine until her mother came home from work. Damn shame when a girl felt safer in the streets, than at her own home. Joe was in the apartment playing video games, smoking weed, eating, and fartin'. That wasn't his job though. His occupation was fuckin' a lonely, over-weight woman, whose self- esteem was low enough to not only accept his behavior, but, sponsor it as well. Joe wasn't quite a plumber, but he was still into 'laying pipe', and getting paid, nonetheless.

"Girl, you crazy!" Jasmine laughed, when she'd arrived home to find her friend sitting in front of her apartment. "You whooped her ass though!"

"Shoot, I got tired of that mutt always messin' with me!" Triste said, as if she hadn't started both fights that day. Kenya had started plenty in her own right, but that day, it had all been Triste's doing.

"Oh, 'bout time you got your damn period. I was starting to think you was one of them 'whatcha ma call it' things like that chic on Love and Hip Hop; the one that messes with that guy who looks like a rat."

"You mean a hermaphrodite?" Triste asked, helping her vocabulary challenged friend. Jasmine was pretty, she was funny, she was loyal, but she definitely wasn't the sharpest tool in the shed, or brightest bulb in the box, or…., let's just say, the girl was dumb.

"Yeah, that's her name!" Jasmine guessed. Anything with more than three syllables may as well have been Korean, as far as she was concerned.

"How long am I gonna be bleeding?" Triste asked with a frown on her face.

"All depends. Mine only lasts' for a couple of days, 'cause I eat a lot of sugar. My momma bleeds for a whole damn week 'cause she likes salt," Jasmine explained.

Still it didn't sound quite right to Triste, so she decided she'd look it up online when she got home; of course, she wouldn't be going home until Janice got home. If Joe would rape her while her mother was at home and right down the hall, what would he do if he ever got her home alone, she wondered.

She waited a few minutes after seeing her mother's car pull up before leaving. She wanted to wait for the weed and alcohol to get into her mother's system first.

"I'm finna' go. You still gonna give me that?"

"Give you what?" Jasmine asked, having forgotten their talk earlier; that, along with everything they'd been taught in school that day.

"You know, the gun? You said you was gonna let me hold one," Triste reminded her. She was too 'green' to realize people didn't borrow guns.

"What you gonna do? Use it and bring it back? Just make sure to fill it back up. Nah, on second thought, you can keep that one."

"Oh, ok. Come one," Jasmine said leading the way to her brother's locked bedroom door. The multiple locks clearly meant nothing to Jasmine. She used a butter knife and an expired bankcard ,and just like that, she was in seconds. "Pick one," she said, opening a drawer filled with guns, condoms, and ammo.

"This one," Triste said, picking a big one. Joe was a big guy, so in her mind, it would take a big gun to kill him.

"Girl, do you know how to use it?" Jasmine asked frowning.

"No, do you?" Triste shot back asking her friend.

"No, but I know where we can learn how!" she said and turned on the TV. She turned to the Rap videos and they both sat down to watch. An hour later, they were both weapon experts and could also make their booties clap. She cocked the gun racking a live round and went home.

"Heard your little period came on and you bled all over your class!" Janice barked, as Triste opened the door to the apartment. That was Janice's way of saying, "hey, baby how was your day?"

"Yes, momma I….."

"Yes momma hell! Get your ass in that kitchen and make dinner! What you think, you a woman now 'cause you got your period?!" Her mother yelled, chasing her into the kitchen. She tried to snuggle up to her man while he played the video game, but had gotten rejected.

"Get off of me! Dang, you made me crash my car!" he grumbled, as if he hadn't been playing the game all day. Truth be told, hearing that his victim was on her period had ruined his plans for the evening. "Shit, I might as well quit playing now!"

"I'm sorry. I just wanted some affection," she pouted sadly. She hopped off the sofa and headed towards the rear of the apartment.

"My bad Shawty, I'ma break you off real good tonight," he promised before she could get away. He figured he may as well since Triste was 'out of order' temporarily.

"OK, I'm gonna go ahead and take a shower." The big woman cheered bouncing up and down like a big bear. Joe never brought in one coin for the house, nor did he bother to fix anything that needed fixing, but he didn't mind 'laying pipe'.

"Yea, make sure you wash that box out real good so I can get me a lil' taste," he called after her. He didn't really like putting his face between her big black thighs, but it was in his job description. Joe had been damn near homeless, sleeping on friends sofa, when he'd caught his latest suga' momma. He preferred the big girls because they were known to pay like they weigh, and of course, they kept plenty of food in the house. When Joe had met Janice he'd talked her huge panties down and put it down on her. It was an audition, job interview, and he had showed out. Her big ass was still shivering as she handed over the keys to her home, and to her child.

"Stop!" Triste whined pitifully as Joe snuck up on her in the kitchen and grabbed her butt. She was so small, both of her small cheeks fit in one of his hands.

"I got my period," she announced looking over at her book bag. If that didn't stop him, she was going to shoot him, right there in the kitchen; Janice too if she didn't like it.

"Period?" Shit, girl that ain't nothin' but a comma. Nothin' but a pause, 'cause as soon as it's over, I'm coming back for some more of that "good stuff," Joe warned her, before slithering away like the snake he was.

"On second thought, I'ma go pretend it's you while I fuck your fat ass mother."

Triste was kept up half the night by Janice's hoopin' and hollerin' from Joe running up in her. She couldn't help but to wonder why Joe even wanted her, since her mother seemed to love it so much.

Abuse or no abuse, Triste like most daughters, adored her mother. She was the only family Triste had and she loved her dearly. She could never figure out why her mother would never return that love. She couldn't figure out why her mother belittled and harassed her. Triste thought her mother's dark skin was beautiful. One day she'd made the mistake of openly admiring her mother, which caused her to receive a hard slap across the face from her mother that was so hard the force knocked her down.

"Fuck you mean you love my black skin? What, you think you better than me 'cause yo' daddy white?! You still a nigga!" Janice screamed down on the confused child.

The next morning, Janice was dancing around like a love struck grizzly. She hummed Anita Baker's song while whipping up a huge breakfast. Triste was happy too, seeing the eggs, bacon and biscuits, while Janice stirred some hash browns. She ignored Joe's lustful gaze and sat down at the table. Her happiness was short-lived when her mother began to divide the feast into two plates.

"Here you go, my long dick, good strokin' king," she said placing a plate piled high in front of Joe. She sat the other plate in front of her and begin to dig in.

"You ain't make me none?" Triste pleaded, on the verge of tears.

"Bitch, did you make me cum four times last night? I don't think so. You better fix you a bowl of cereal and get the fuck out my face!"

Triste was too mad to eat now. She got up and stormed out of the kitchen and apartment, ignoring her mother's ranting behind her back, as she walked away. Just like the proverbial straw that had broken the camel's back, that was the 'dis' that had broken Triste's heart, made a big hole in it, and all the love she'd had for her mother slipped out of it.

"I hate that bitch!" she finally admitted to herself.

******

Joe's sick ass had been monitoring Triste's period by keeping up with the amount of pads in the garbage can. She was so self-conscious about her first period, that she pushed the discarded pads as deep into the garbage can as possible, but not too deep for Joe's nasty ass, who had gone in after them. He checked her 'flow' daily.

"Oh, it's back on tomorrow," he announced when he came across a pad that was almost clean of any traces of Triste's blood. Now, it was his turn to dance around the apartment with glee. Triste knew why he was so happy. It didn't matter because her mind was already made up. If he touched her again, she was going to kill him.

Murder would be a tough act for her to digest, so she decided to try talking to her mother one more time. She was her mother after all; surely she would protect her child. Even animals care for their young. Hearing her mother cackling on the phone, Triste held out on what she had to say for a minute, so she wouldn't interrupt her. She also did a little ear hustling while she waited for her mother's attention.

"Girl, I'm so sick of this yellow bitch, I don't know what to do!" Janice said to her friend who was on the other end of the phone. "I swear, I'ma end up droppin' this little heifer back off to the Foster Care Center and let them keep this check! No wonder her real momma ain't wanna keep her! Oh, girl, let me tell you, lil' miss thang had the nerve to try and tell me my man been touchin' on her! Like somebody really would want her lil' narrow ass! You should see the way this bitch be walkin' around here like she 'all that'!"

Triste was blinded by the tears and rage as she walked away. First, she walked into the wall as she retreated, then she accidently walked right into Joe.

"Whoa, lil' momma," Joe said when she bumped into him. He took the opportunity to rub her budding breasts'. When he got no resistance, he reached around to feel her butt. If Janice wasn't at home, he would've raped her right then and there.

"What the fuck is going on out here?" Janice screamed, when she walked up on them and saw Joe touching Triste. Triste was so relieved that he'd been caught in the act, a smile formed on her face. She immediately got punched in the face knocking the short-lived smile right off.

"Bitch, you in here rubbin' your lil' ass on my man's hands!" Janice yelled and kicked the fallen child. She stomped on the girl as if she was on fire.

"Chill baby, I'm OK," Joe said pulling her away. "Why don't you roll us up a blunt and let me get you a beer."

"OK baby," Janice huffed, winded from the expenditure of energy. "I saw that lil' bitch touchin' you and I couldn't help but go crazy!" "I know, I know," he said leading her to their bedroom. Once he he'd gotten her settled down, he went to go and spike her beer. He had a hot date planned for the night.

******

"You ready for me?" Joe asked seductively while he stood in Triste's bedroom door. He actually leaned against the frame in a sexy pose.

Killa

CHRONICLES OF A STICK UP KID

Introduction

Xing Lee was talking cash shit as the good doctor stroked away at her hairless box. She was 'oohing' and 'aahing' and cursing in her native tongue as her current lover loved her. For all he knew she was talking bad about him but he didn't speak Vietnamese so it sounded as good as it felt.

"Me love you long time!" Doc grunted as he slammed into her. His love life had greatly improved since his miserable wife died at the hands of the country's most dangerous killer known as Killa.

The doctor was treated as a hero after surviving the home invasion that claimed his beloved wife. A minor celebrity to all except his wife's family. They blamed him for his former patient taking her life.

Doc now had quite a few girlfriends on payroll, but Xing was by far his favorite. He currently had her on her side in the 'scissor' position and was giving her the business. He was four and a half inches deep pounding away. His prim and prissy wife would have never let him put her in a position like this. Whenever she did feel benevolent enough to part with a little vagina it was one way, from the back while laying on her side so she wouldn't have to look at him. There was no kissing, no talking or tenderness. Just hurry up and get off and get off.

When the doctor's stroke grew choppy, Xing threw it into overdrive. She began moaning and thrashing around as if he was slaying it. He wasn't, she was just a good actor. Her performance helped doc reach an intense orgasm he no doubt would tip for.

Xing was bright enough to at least let her lover think he was knocking it out the park. The key to a man's heart is his ego, not stomach. Any stranger can fill your belly, but making a middle aged man feel vibrant was more important. She may or may not have had an orgasm along with him. It's hard to tell with professionals, or wives.

"Ooh doctor you number one G.I! You love me long time!" Xing said quite believably as she got up from the bed. She rushed into the bathroom and under the shower. She was back minutes later and quickly dressed. A kiss on the forehead served as goodbye, and she was gone.

"I'm an animal!" Doc cheered, beating on his chest like King Kong. It's one of the silly things people do when they think they're alone, only he wasn't.

"Lion or tiger?" a voice asked from the shadows.

Ordinarily the ordinary man would have been frightened at the presence of an uninvited stranger in his home, but he wasn't. He actually smiled at the sound of a voice he knew well. Uninvited he may have been, but he was no stranger.

"A lion, I'm king of the fucking jungle!" he laughed as his now welcome guest stepped from the shadows and into view. "How long have you been here?"

"Long enough to see you and your buddy bumping uglies. Oh, and I speak Korean. She was saying you have a little dick and your elbow was pulling her hair."

"Fuck you Killa, she's Vietnamese!" Doc laughed cracking them both up. "Let me put something on."

228

Killa turned away when the doctor bounded out of the bed in his pinkish birthday suit.

"You're looking trim, no homo," he complimented.

"None taken, thank you," doc said proudly as he headed into his bathroom to wash his and Xing's body fluids off of him. When he returned he found the room empty. He almost called out in fear until he smelled his guest in the other room. Killer had found his way to the den and poured a shot of cognac to go along with his blunt. Doc found him laying back in a recliner blowing smoke rings from the pungent weed.

"So, what brings you back to town? I assumed you would be in Brazil or Belize by now. It's been what, a year?" the doctor asked as he poured a shot of his own.

"Back? Shit I never left. I love Atlanta" Killa replied. He extended the blunt to his host out of courtesy, and to his surprise the doctor took it and took a healthy pull.

"A lot's changed," Killa said noting the new life in the older man.

"Well yeah! I've changed everything," the doctor replied between tokes. He assumed Killa meant the new decor of the house, not his new demeanor. The weight loss, the tan, the, weed smoking it took his wife's death for him to live.

"I feel like a new man, I'm alive!" doc cheered.

"Yeah well murder will do that. Why you think I'm always so fucking happy" Killa chuckled.

"Been killing much?" doc asked enthusiastically.

"Have I!" he shot back animatedly at the gross understatement.

"Tell me about it, please!" the doctor gushed eagerly and adjusted himself to get comfortable for the ride. He leaned back on his chaise to enjoy the story totally unaware he would be a part of it.

The Preacher's Wife

Prologue

How the hell did I get here? Teresa wondered inwardly as she glanced up at the giggling teenager standing over her.

If the act wasn't bad enough, she also had to contend with the young man's vulgar speech and sweaty balls slapping at her chin.

"Dats right! Suck dat dick bitch! Eat it hoe!" Lil Red demanded as he humped her face. Technically it couldn't be called a blow job because the vile little boy was literally fucking her face.

Teresa gagged loudly each time he slammed into her larynx. Her full mouth forced her to inhale the flavor of nuts that had missed at least two showers, and in the sweltering Atlanta heat that's not a good idea.

"*Just hurry,*" Teresa sighed, "*And do not... cu.... Ewww! He's coming in my mouth!*"

"Mmm take it bitch! Eat! Eat!" Lil Red giggled as he skeeted on her tonsils. Teresa had no choice but to swallow the pulses of bitter semen since her head was held firmly in place.

"Dayum you got some fire ass head!" The man child exclaimed, taking a few final humps before extracting himself from her mouth.

"Thank you, you're too kind," Teresa replied sarcastically but the quip was wasted on the ignorant young dealer.

"Here you go shawty," Lil Red said, extending his open palm filled with dime size pieces of crack. The young veteran had cut the drug at angles that made it appear more than it actually was. Still, five dimes was a lot for some head.

The local junkies will go as low as four dollars in a pinch. But this was no local junky. Her SUV, clothes, and even her smell spoke money, yet she had none. Lil Red didn't think she would accept his crass proposal to "suck a nigga dick" but she did.

Teresa looked at the drugs with dismay. She felt like slapping the poison across the room. However, a far more intense urge insisted she pluck them from his hand.

"Shit fall through tomorrow, I'll let you suck this dick again," Lil Red offered politely over his shoulder as he exited the hotel room.

As soon as he crossed the threshold of the door, Teresa ran to secure it. She loathed the ghetto of Atlanta, but crack cocaine was not sold in her upscale suburban neighborhood.

She quickly removed one of the rocks from its tiny plastic bag and spilt it in two. After loading one half onto her straight shooter, she quickly followed it up with a flame.

'*Ahhh!*'Teresa exclaimed when she finally exhaled that overdue hit. She deserved it too for all she does. Daughter Hazel was at ballet class and son Calvin was at soccer, this was "me time".

Her free hours were spent devouring the drugs she purchased with her dignity. Then it was time to return to her life, "Life as the Preachers Wife."

CHAPTER 1

Teresa Sanders was born Teresa McCoy in Atlanta, at Grady Hospital thirty five Christmas days ago. Complications ensured she would be the couple's only child.

Her parents reigned over a mid-sized church on Atlanta's south west side. The first Baptist Church of Christ was located on busy Cascade Ave. The congregation consisted entirely of the middle class home owners in the area. They tithed generously to the church and to pastor McCoy personally.

They made sure he had a new car every year 'cuz pastor can't be seen driving no bullshit.' The church even gifted the family the biggest house in the area.

The income allowed the McCoy's to lavish their child with gifts and special treatment that spoiled the pretty little girl rotten. By three years old, Teresa was not only use to having her way she actually demanded it.

"NO" was a word totally foreign to the Prima Donna. She was prone to world class tantrums if not given her way. At times the brat would insist upon items she didn't really desire. This was done to ensure a garage laden with unwanted novelties that no longer held her interest.

Teresa was a beautiful baby, then a pretty little girl. By high school she was drop dead gorgeous. She even inherited her mom's wide hips and fat ass that had hooked her daddy many years back. Hands down she was the prettiest girl in any room she walked into.

Her parents enrolled her in all girls' schools in attempt to keep dicks out of their child. By high school they had enrolled her in a prestigious Christian Academy. The sky high tuition, they felt would keep the riff raff away. Yes, the McCoy's were naïve enough to believe money meant class and sophistication.

Why they thought this environment would be any safer morally than anywhere else is a mystery. Sure they were free from the violence that plagues the inner city schools. However, all those sexually repressed girls in the same place was just as dangerous. It created a sexual energy comparable only to the sun.

Sex was the topic of the day, every day, all day. There were even a few lesbian couples who dated discreetly. They figured same sex was better than no sex.

Most of the staff at the school was female. The idea was to create a no dick environment, a green zone if you will. The few males who did work there were filtered by unattractiveness and thoroughly screened. They all passed background checks, even Coach Jenkins.

Mathew Jenkins was a twenty three year old recent grad of a Bible college. He was a junior pastor at one of Atlanta's mega churches and had excellent references. His only flaw was being a hunk.

He was so handsome; he almost didn't get the job. Even the head administrator got a little moist during the interview. Finding no other, or no ugly suitable substitute male or female, Coach Jenkins was hired.

All the girls as well as half of the staff flirted shamelessly with the well-built P.E. instructor. Coach, however was far too upright pious and honest to return the interest shown to him. He was superman, until Teresa came along shaking her kryptonite.

"Lord have mercy!" He exclaimed when he saw Teresa stretching her hamstrings before class. The first things he noticed were her big brown legs. She looked like she could leap a building in a single bound.

A pretty morsel of ass-cheek protruded from the tiny school issued shorts. When she stood upright her full breast made the words "Christian Academy" on the shirt look like a billboard.

Not only was he hard as a diamond from gawking at the girl but found himself being propelled towards her.

"Excuse me young lady," he began cautiously, "When you stretch don't bounce. Slow ..... and .... Easy," he demonstrated.

"Oh okay, thanks!" Teresa gushed, thankful for the advice as well as a chance to see the man who had all the girls buzzing up close and personal.

"Like this?" she asked, as she slowly bent at the waist until she was touching her toes.

"Let me see," he said sliding behind her to get a good view of her round ass. "Perfect!"

The private lesson came to an abrupt end as the other girls began filing out the locker room. The session was over, but the last lustful gaze they shared said something else had begun. The seeds were sown.

Coach and student bantered playfully every chance they got. The mutual attraction grew into intense staring matches charged with sexual tones. It was now just a matter of time. The only thing keeping him out of the girl was opportunity. She was as good as fucked first chance he got.

Teresa was conflicted between her upbringing and her desires. She had fully intended on saving herself for her future husband, but now that was in question. Coach soaked her panties daily with his deep voice and brown eyes. The occasional brush against each other that they managed made her vagina throb.

She wasn't alone in her frustration. Coach had been an athlete in high school and had plenty of girls. Halfway through college he put his dick away picked up the Bible and vowed celibacy. Now he found himself masturbating after an encounter with the young stunner.

Yep, just a matter of time. Neither were surprised when a date was finally planned. It wasn't a date in the traditional sense. He would not come calling on her at home to meet the parents. They just arranged to be in the same place at the same time.

Totally harmless, right?

CHAPTER 2

Reverend McCoy was gifted a brand new Cadillac around the time of Teresa's extravagant sweet sixteen party.

She frowned at the offer of his slightly used vehicle. She claimed that "it was so last years." Her doting father chided himself for being insensitive and quickly traded it for a new convertible.

Even with her own car, Teresa's movements were still monitored closely. Her comings and goings were verified by phone and GPS. Dad knew his daughter was fine and saw the reactions men gave her. He even had to check a couple of deacons about looking at her ass.

Not to mention he was quite the dicks-man himself at that age. He bedded half the neighborhood including his, then sixteen year old, wife. Momma was a little easier to maneuver around, so that's who Teresa tried.

"Momma I'm fixing to go to the mall and meet up with some friends," Teresa sang, lying to her mother for the first time. Since she had such a stellar record her mother eagerly accepted the half-truth.

"Ok, have fun, drive safe and…?"

"No boys!" Teresa laughed

At least that part was true. Mathew was a man not a boy.

Teresa parked her car on the absolute outskirts of the malls huge parking lot. This was to give her a little privacy as she pulled off the loose fitting pants she wore and wiggled into the skin tight pair she brought along. She then pulled off the sweatshirt revealing the tight tee that revealed her breast.

A cursory check in the rearview mirror confirmed that her mid-back length hair was still perfect. Only then was the top lowered as she cruised around to the mall's valet parking to make her grand entrance.

Every male head turned as she sashayed into the mall. The attention was surprising as men married, single, young, old, straight and gay stared. A few of the younger more assertive guys made advances, but they fell upon deaf ears. Teresa only had eyes for one man, and there he was at the food court right on time.

"Wow! You look great!" Coach exclaimed taking her hands and planting a kiss on her cheek. It was the first time a man had ever touched her causing her to flinch.

"I'm sorry," Mathew apologized fearfully as he misunderstood the reaction. "I... just..."

"No I'm fine! No problem, you look great too." Teresa smiled as she regained her composure. She wanted to go wring out her panties but didn't. Instead she tipped toed up and returned the gesture.

The plan was to catch the DOPE BOY movie at two o-clocks so they headed to the mall's theater. With thirty minutes to spare coach led her into the arcade.

"Win me a prize!" Teresa demanded as she would her parents.

"Sure!" Mathew agreed eagerly. Just like her parents. He slid a dollar into the game releasing miniature basketballs. The athlete banked shot after shot into the small goal until the timer ran out.

"Here you try," He offered as a row of tickets slid out of the machine.

"I can't do that," Teresa giggled as her date guided her to the machine. She was far too prissy to shoot hoops but decided to try it for him.

Another dollar was inserted, releasing the balls and starting the timer. She missed every shot, getting more and more frustrated.

"Something must be wrong with the game!" she insisted, "It's either rigged or broken."

"No, it's your technique. Here let me show you."

Like any coach he put his arms around her. He pressed his body against hers, his arms against hers, and helped her shoot hoops.

Teresa casually leaned her ass onto the erection slowly growing towards her and began gyrating. Even after the buzzer had sounded, announcing the end of the game, they lingered until an impatient adolescent demanded they move along.

Coach bought her everything she pointed at in the movie's concession stand. She had no plans on eating the majority of it but ordered it anyway. Once inside the darken theater she slipped her hand inside his.

Neither were able to fully concentrate on Killa Cam on the big screen, as they were both distracted by the others' hand. Even after the movie had ended they maintained their hand holding while they exited the mall. It wasn't until after the valet delivered her car that she released his hand.

"So?" she asked nervously awaiting being told what to do. Secretly she wished he would lean down and kiss her again, but on the lips this time.

She got her wish, Coach gave her, her first kiss. It was soft, sweet, and witnessed.

"Sho-nuff?" Margie exclaimed as she saw her co-worker kiss a student. 'No wonder he's running from me,' she thought.

She had been offering her services to Coach from the second he began working there. Not services actually, she wanted to fuck him.

She assumed that Teresa must be the reason he didn't take the bait. It wasn't. Margie looked like a shaved baboon wearing a horse costume that was the reason.

A wave of emotions swept through her body when his lips touched hers. The strange feeling overwhelmed Teresa causing her to flee.

"I have to go!" She whined and rushed into her car. She sped out of the parking lot and onto the freeway. Finally she slowed down at the sight of a police cruiser in front of her. A huge grin slowly spread on her face as she calmed down. She fondly recalled the feel of the stiff dick on her back.

A million conflicting thoughts battled for attention in her mind until she found herself pulling into her driveway.

"Hey daddy!" she beamed at her father, as he backed his car out of the large driveway. He smiled and waved back. He was heading out to handle the affairs of the church. Pun intended, she parked the car and skipped into the back door.

"Hey momma!" she sang planting a sideways kiss on her mother's pretty face.

"Hey yourself," Mary smiled, turned, then frowned. "Chile did you go out in those tight pants!"

After the close call Teresa decided to keep her distance from Coach. Every time their eyes met she quickly snatched her gaze away. The memory of his touch refused to die that easily. She was in agony every time she saw him.

Coach gave up after a couple of days and backed off. Once he caught her alone he finally spoke.

"Look, I'm sorry if I offended you. The kiss was out of line," He offered sounding sincere.

"Oh, don't be! You've done nothing wrong," Teresa replied. She meant to be stoic and blunt but got caught in his gaze. "It's just... I um... you know we can't...I need to see you again!"

"Come to my apartment!" Coach blurted out surprising even himself. He knew she was a minor, even though age of sexual consent is sixteen. Still with him being her teacher sex would be felonious.

"Let's both play hooky tomorrow," Teresa readily agreed. He almost said "No" and moved on with his life, but almost doesn't count, especially when it comes to statutory rape. It would be futile to say "well your honor I 'almost' didn't fuck her".

That night the junior pastor pulled out all the stops to prevent going through with the plans. He prayed, read his Bible, even spoke in tongues. Nothing worked to subdue his lustful desires. He couldn't even masturbate it away. And he tried that too.

In the end he decided to send her straight to school if she showed up at his apartment. That was until he pulled the door open the next morning. He took one look at her and ushered her inside.

Teresa rushed straight into his arms and kissed him. She had been up late contemplating the situation as well. The verdict was that her virginity was for her one day husband, but Coach could touch her if he wanted to. She may even touch him back. But that would be it, no intercourse.

Everything between entering the apartment and lying naked on Mathew's bed was a blur.

CPSIA information can be obtained
at www.ICGtesting.com
Printed in the USA
LVHW040306030123
736289LV00005B/526